I0525113

SoulTaker

ALSO BY JERRY MAPLES

The Divine Discovery

Divine Misguidance

Covert Crossing

Patient 22

SoulTaker

Jerry Maples

Ms. Tree Publishing
Tempe, Arizona

Copyright © 2022-23 by Jerry Maples

First U.S. Edition 2022

10 9 8 7 6 5 4 3 2 1

ISBN: 978-09759816-4-1

Cover design by Carol Skewes

All rights reserved. No part of this publication may be reproduced, stored in, or introduced into a retrieval system, or transmitted in any form, or by any means (electronic, mechanical, photocopying, recording, or otherwise) without the prior written permission of both the copy right owner and the publisher of this book.

This book is a work of fiction. Names, characters, businesses, organizations, places, events, and incidents either are the product of the author's imagination or are used fictitiously. Any resemblance to actual persons, living or dead, events, or locales is entirely coincidental.

Ms. Tree Publishing
2645 E. Southern Ave., A-683
Tempe, AZ 85282

Printed in the United States of America

CHAPTER ONE
October 22

The handsome twenty-six-year-old fearfully entered Manuel's Bar located in San Francisco's warehouse district near his uncle's office. He had hated arranging this meeting, but realized there was no choice but to inform Rafa of what had happened at work this morning.

Adjusting his eyes to California's glaring sun, Diego Reyes squinted as he entered the dim interior. Instantly he heard a familiar gruff bark, "Over here, Dee." There was a touch of irritation in his uncle's voice. "What's so damn important we have to meet in the middle of the day? I've got a ton of shipments that have to go out by six."

Uncle Rafa didn't appreciate being interrupted from his frenzied morning. He was hoping to avoid the ire of his boss who masterminded the Los Lomas drug operation. For over forty years in the Sinaloa cartel, Rafa had been El Jefe's number one man and he didn't want to screw up things during his last few months until retirement. Starting as an enforcer of drug distribution, he had risen through the ranks to land the plush job of running the San Francisco center responsible for supplying drugs to the entire northwest US. His major misfortune occurred twenty years earlier when he took part in a shootout resulting in the death of his brother-in-law. Ironically that incident had a provident aspect because it led to adopting his nephew and shielding the boy from growing up in the dangerous business. The two had grown close with Diego developing a promising career in neurology at the Jobs Institute of Technology.

Passing by two men seated at an adjacent table, Diego received nods of recognition. This was a familiar haunt for meetings with his uncle. Approaching Rafa, he wiped his sweaty hands on his khakis to avoid revealing his anxiety. *God, I hate to tell him how I screwed up. I was so stupid. But it's best to come out with it and get it over.* Exhaling deeply, he sank onto the bar stool afraid to make eye contact with his kin.

Uncle Rafa raised his eyebrows and asked, "You look like you just saw a ghost. What's up? Thought we weren't going to meet until after work."

Bracing himself for a brutal response, the nephew blurted out, "I lost my job."

"What? Whaddaya mean 'lost your job'?" Being there is vital to making your scheme work. What are you going to do now?"

"I've got another way. I can still keep up with how the project's going."

"Jesus, Son, we've already got our necks stretched out a mile. Your solution better be a good one." Rafa leaned his huge hulk forward as if moving closer would help in learning something positive.

Diego began to relate the situation. "You always warned me to keep my pecker in my pants. Well, I couldn't help it. The situation came about when we were testing Luke's device on the most erotic-looking co-ed I've ever seen. The laser was focused on her cortex and we were exchanging messages through thought waves. Then Luke was called away. So, I continued without him. That was when she started sending me dirty messages. Saying things like 'I'm horny' and 'Could we go to bed sometime soon?' She really turned me on. I got hard and, you know me, I had to do something about it. Well, before I knew it, I leaped across the table and started ripping off her shirt. That's when Luke came back. He saw me groping her.

He whacked the laser across the room. And I saw horror in her eyes. At that point the damned pussy pouted I was taking advantage of her. I've never seen his rage like I did then. She yelled that if I wasn't fired, she'd raise holy hell. I saw Luke feared this could put an end to his invention. So, he terminated me on the spot."

During the explanation Rafa's face became so red it seemed like he was about to explode.

Diego raised a hand attempting to calm the situation. Then he said, "Luke had no choice but to fire me. But it still won't stop me from stealing his invention. That thing is worth a fortune. We'll be able to communicate with others through thought waves. They won't have any idea how we're getting into their mind. Just imagine, we'll be able to influence their thinking and make them do things. The power this gives us is incredible."

"Yeah," Rafa replied, "but since you don't work there anymore, how will you know he's got it done so you can take it."

"Maria will keep me posted."

Grimacing, Rafa thought about it. After anticipating what Diego would say, his composure relaxed and he said, "Okay, Kid."

"Luke is only a couple of months away from finishing the fine tuning. Once that's done, I'll steal it."

"Fine tuning? The way you talked the other day, I thought it was ready to go."

"Well, it basically is. Our tests are showing the subjects willingly cooperate and they no longer experience any ill effects. Previous headaches and trauma have been virtually eliminated. The information they're giving us is unbelievable. Not only can we access whatever they're thinking, but they cooperate in sharing memories and experiences. Maybe it'll even help them remember things they seem to have forgotten. Luke's created a hell of an invention."

In the past year as Luke's assistant, Diego learned how to operate the system. But he could only do this when Luke opened the device by inputting the secret algorithm. His boss would not share the code because he believed a subject's information should remain private. While findings could be beneficial to the subject or for psychological research, Luke had feared the data gathered might be used for nefarious purposes.

The more Diego became familiar with operating Luke's invention the more he understood the capabilities it possessed. He saw that operating the device could give one incredible power to access a person's private data, knowledge and experiences. With his devious mindset, Diego began to imagine ways he could financially gain by controlling the SoulTaker. Several weeks earlier he mentioned this to Rafa who, after some thought, came up with a bizarre idea. Partnering with a company having global connections could lead to finding a buyer willing to pay millions for the device. That was when he mentioned this to the boss of his cartel.

After Diego reported on the status of Luke's device, his uncle said, "Things are going well on my end, too. When I told El Jefe about all the money we could make on this deal, he got so excited he shared the news with Colombia." Rafa was referring to the Medellin cartel, Sinaloa's primary supplier of drugs to the world. "Now they want in on the deal. Said this could bring in a hell of a lot of money. When they considered using it for blackmail and espionage, its value was out of sight. So big in fact, they want to be the major player and put together a group that could pay us millions. Seems like the buyers might be Iran and North Korea in a joint venture. . . Well nephew, how do you like them apples?"

The beam on the uncle's face reflected his never-ending desire to be important.

Diego gulped but said nothing. *Jesus, Uncle. Are we getting into something over our heads? After everyone else takes their cut, will there be anything left for us? Besides, knowing what I do about the Colombians, if we screw up, we could be toast.*

CHAPTER TWO

February 12

Since six o'clock this Thursday morning Luke Pope had been chained to his desk in the neurology lab at Jobs Institute of Technology (JIT) in Palo Alto, California. He groaned slightly as he stood to stretch his legs. He attributed their dull ache to his six-foot-seven-inch stature when the problem was actually an aversion to exercise. For most of his life, he had rationalized there was little time for exercise or anything else but to concentrate on the challenge of learning. That was his number one priority in life. For more than two decades his energies had been focused on knowing whatever he could about the human brain. Now he planned to devote his energies to create advances that were on the leading edge of science.

Recently, this was a very special time for him because the drive to succeed had ratcheted up another notch. He was in the final stages of creating an invention that would enable people to communicate with one another through the exchange of thought waves. The feedback from testing student volunteers reflected this could be done with little or no adverse effects when being bombarded by the laser beams emitted from his device. The notoriety and lucrative arrangements with industry due to this invention could vault JIT to an elite status in science. In fact, the university's board of regents had put Luke's project on the fast track despite still having to resolve some minor neurological dangers to the students being tested.

While exercising his legs he had surveyed the lab's cramped area that served as its lobby and reception area. This consisted mainly of a workstation with computers, electronic equipment, and an accompanying laser apparatus. The laser device was comprised of two parts: the transmitter, a revolver-like gun to emit the laser rays, plus the receiver/recorder for returning the subject's response to the operator.

When the lanky scientist returned to his office chair, he removed his eyeglasses and proceeded to rub his eyes. Their dryness felt as though they were coated with sandpaper.

Luke bubbled with excitement as he reviewed the results of the volunteer interviews he had conducted. Based on exit interviews of the participants, he discovered his latest fine-tuning adjustments exceeded expectations. He had also been experimenting with ways to implant ideas in the subject's mind. Once the subject received the sender's message, his thoughts were automatically transmitted back without the subject being aware of it.

In his testing, Luke discovered the participants usually expressed disbelief they were exchanging information. But after some coaxing, they understood what was happening and soon felt at ease in relaying their thoughts. As a result, Luke was able to get into the mind of a subject and explore whatever he desired. This process worked as long as they remained within a line-of-sight connection of the laser beam.

For more than six months, feedback from the volunteers participating in the tests revealed most of the bugs had been resolved. There were no longer incidents of head trauma. A jubilant smile formed on the neurologist's face knowing his creation was nearly complete.

Just then, a tap on his office door interrupted his reflections. A frail-looking person with easy-going mannerisms entered and settled into the chair next to his desk. The appearance of Phil gave Luke a warm and comfortable feeling. At the age of ten, Luke had been adopted by his neighbor Phillip Abbott who raised him in a loving home environment. The two developed a strong bond immediately and young Luke followed in his adoptive father's footsteps by studying in the same field. Ten years later the pair reunited when Luke joined Phillip who directed the neurology department at Jobs Institute of Technology (JIT). In their two years of working together, Luke was allowed to concentrate his energies exclusively on research due to his creativity.

"Good morning, Luke," Phil said. "I've got some good news for you."

"Good morning, Phil, I have something to tell you, too. But you first."

Abbott excitedly blurted, "Last night I got a text from Trey!"

Trey was the CEO of a mega pharmaceutical firm located in San Diego. The name of this company, CM3, was a tribute to himself: Sterling Claymore III. Although exceptionally bright and driven, the owner had a reputation for being egotistical, bombastic, and a riverboat gambler. His humongous stature was topped off with a ridiculous toupee. The man was a legend, a third-generation entrepreneur born with a silver spoon in his mouth.

Phillip continued, "I've scheduled him for a demo."

Luke bolted upright in his chair and replied, "What? What do you mean?"

"Sterling Claymore wants to see your SoulTaker. Thinks he could market it nationwide and make a lot of money for both of us. If it's as good as the assistant he lent you said, he'd like to do a joint venture with us."

Trey's assistant had been on loan to Luke for nearly four months. Prior to that time, word had spread throughout the scientific community about Luke Pope's creativity. And when Trey learned Luke had fired his previous assistant, he immediately offered a temporary replacement. That way, the CEO hoped to have the inside track in marketing the SoulTaker and becoming its exclusive distributor.

Phil was excited. "He's offering a thirty-million-dollar donation to JIT."

Luke's eyes flashed with excitement.

Phil continued, "Now he wants to know how long will it be before he can see a demo."

"That's terrific, Phil. I'm hoping to have it ready in a week or two. Here, look at this." He flipped him a print-out of the testing results. "The data shows how accurate we are in communicating through thought waves. But before I let any prospective investor see a demonstration, we've got a major problem to work out. That's how do we resolve the ethical problem before it's brought to market?"

His boss solemnly nodded, along with a look that signaled he was not going to be pleased.

Luke continued, "My volunteers are convinced that the SoulTaker is an incredible advancement. But my problem is allowing anyone's mind to be invaded without their being aware. This is an invasion of their privacy. And I cannot be a party to that. . . Phil, just imagine what this device could do to our society if it got in the wrong hands. Nothing could remain confidential anymore. A person would have no secrets. Besides, that person might even be brainwashed or have ideas implanted in their mind. I'm not going to let that happen."

Phil replied, "Well, until you get that fixed, you'll have to do something like we talked about. . . You know, use an algorithm."

Luke nodded.

The two had previously discussed one way to limit this problem. Require a specific code to be entered into the device in order for the system to operate. Then, with Luke keeping the algorithm to himself, no one else could run the device.

Phil said, "Let's put a hold on solving that problem. Getting Trey's thirty-million-dollars would be a Godsend for the university. Could we agree to his request and show him a demo by the end of next week?"

"Well, I'm sure I can have it ready by then."

"Okay, I'll tell him that's your plan," Phil replied. "We can't miss his generous offer."

"The only problem is, first I need a break. I've been working my ass off. I'm exhausted and stressed out. What I really need is some time off to recharge my batteries. When I return Monday, I'll be re-energized and hit it with a vengeance. Okay?"

His boss gave a sour look but relented because he had promised to set a date for the demo. Then, after observing Luke's steely-eyed glare, his frown turned into a slight smile. "Sure, you deserve it."

"Don't worry Phil. I'll have plenty of time to make sure everything is in order."

CHAPTER THREE

January 27

It was the middle of the evening when Luke received an unexpected visitor at his home. This was three weeks earlier, before Luke had agreed to perform the demo for Sterling Claymore. As he went to answer the buzz at his front door, what the neurologist spied on his porch caused him to gasp.

"Hello Diego," he said, motioning his former assistant to come in. "I thought I had seen the last of you when I fired you a couple of months ago."

"Yeah, it seems like a long time. I am so sorry for throwing a tantrum. And I've been too embarrassed to give you my apology." Actually, for Diego, this wasn't the truth of his visit. He had been out of the loop in SoulTaker's development and had heard from his lover Maria that the final problems were about to be resolved. His strategy was to steal the device as soon as that happened. And a key part of this plan was to set up Luke for being kidnapped. What he needed now was to persuade Luke to contact a woman who would then entice him to leave town where he could be more easily abducted.

"Well come in. Why don't you join me for a cup of tea and tell me what you've been up to."

As Luke ushered Diego to a chair, he said, "I've missed having you at the lab. You always kept me on my toes with your constant questions. How're you doing?"

The guest returned a sheepish look. Then looking away, he settled in the easy chair, slumping his shoulders, saying, "Luke, I'm terribly sorry for treating you the way I did. You still remain a good friend."

"Gee thanks," the neurologist replied reflecting a quizzical look. "For a while I felt you were really pissed at me. You know I had no choice but to let you go in order to preserve the integrity of the SoulTaker project. You should never have sexually attacked that co-ed."

"Yeah, I understand. Sometimes I just can't control my urges." Then continuing to avoid eye contact, Diego began to spin a lie hoping to get back into Luke's good graces. "The real problem is I've been under a lot of stress. . . A family problem. But I really didn't mean to take it out on you. Still, I'm here to ask for your forgiveness."

"What happened?"

"My uncle's got a health problem. It came on so sudden. He's always been in good condition. Kept the matter to himself. Then, I learned he has pancreatic cancer. Stage four. It happened without any warning. I took it tough. You know he was a father to me. . . I was mad at God, but decided to stay home to take care of him. Neither of us have any close relatives."

"Yeah, I know. . . How's he doing now?"

"Not good. He needs a lot of help."

"I'm so sorry Diego. Is there anything I can do for you?"

"Naw. Just keep him in your prayers." It was ironic because everyone knew Luke was an outspoken atheist. What was meant to be silly came out tacky. After a moment, Diego regained his composure. "I feel crappy about ruining our relationship. I've waited too long to fill you in on why I acted so poorly. And I wanted to somehow make up for being such a shit."

"Don't worry about it. You were a good partner and helped get my project off the ground. You probably don't know, but things are going well."

Diego was aware of that. The first part of his plan involved his clandestine lover, Maria Gonzalez. Months ago, Diego had convinced Robin, the third member of Luke's team, to share her apartment with Maria. Robin had been working for the JIT Neurology department and when Luke took over the neurology research lab, she was hired to be his assistant. Later when Diego joined the group, he became aware of the closeness of his two workmates and realized there might come a time when Robin could be used as a buffer in his relationship with Luke. Fortunately, due to Maria's relationship with Robin, she was able to keep him posted on current developments with Luke's invention. This brilliant arrangement came in handy when Diego made the mistake of being fired. Maria loved him so much she would do anything to keep her lover happy.

The key info Luke kept to himself was the algorithm needed to open the SoulTaker. He had become paranoid about sharing this code with anyone. Consequently no one else could operate the system. On those times Diego was allowed to run the system, it was only after Luke secretly entered the code. Finally, in desperation, Diego figured the only way to operate the SoulTaker was to abduct Luke and force him to give up the code. So, with the help of Rafa, he found a woman who would set up a kidnapping by asking Luke out on a date.

Diego recalled in his months of working with Luke that the man missed spending time with a woman. His divorce two years earlier, when combined with being such an introvert, compounded his need for rare times of companionship. Diego decided to use this situation to fan the flames, "Luke, to show my remorse for treating you so badly, I have a special present for you. I'm giving you the name of a woman that would love to spend Valentine's weekend with you. I guarantee she's someone who will satisfy your every sexual fantasy."

Instinctively, Luke's eyes bugged out and his mouth dropped open. "Wha—wha—what are you talking about?"

"I've already contacted her and she's a go. You can thank me later. Send a message to Krystal telling her you're a friend of mine. Here's her address." After handing it over, he continued, "Ask her to set up a date and she'll take care of arranging everything. All I ask is that you keep this just between the two of us."

As soon as it was convenient Diego left Luke's home with a devilish smile on his face and a bounce in his step. He could hardly wait to share the good news with his uncle.

CHAPTER FOUR

February 17

It was the Monday after Valentine's Day, when Robin Hunt arrived early at the neurology lab. This week was to be the culmination of introducing Luke's latest invention to the world.

Robin had been told to report an hour earlier than normal to prepare for the fine tuning. Both she and Scott were expected to be ready by 7 a.m. A glance at her watch showed it was almost 6:30. Being prepared ahead of time was normal for her. She had even managed to complete her normal first task of each day: Bring Luke his special drink from the Dutch Brothers Coffee Shop. She accepted the fact that this was one of the ways to exercise control. After working two years for Luke, she had grown accustomed to his idiosyncrasies.

This lithe, buxom brunette took a moment to reflect on the good fortune of finding this career. The opportunity came about strictly by accident. Every moment of her first meeting with Luke was etched into her memory. It happened one morning while rushing late to her job. She experienced a glancing blow from his Camaro while jaywalking through a university parking lot. Although the bump was at a slow speed, it caused her to collapse onto the pavement. Coming to her senses, she found herself spread-eagled on the sidewalk with a man towering above her. Her first thought was: *My what a good-looking man. And he's so tall, too.* In her slightly dazed condition, she batted her big brown eyes at him as she said, "Sorry, it was my fault."

Luke replied, "I... I hope you're okay." Not knowing what else to say, he offered her a hand and tenderly helped her to her feet. A grin formed on his face when he noticed she was tall like him, guessing her to be around six-foot-three.

"Don't worry about me, mister. I'm all right. Looks like you were in quite a hurry."

"Yeah, I'm late for a meeting. . .Er. . . er . . .Well, I'm not going to leave you like this. Can you walk?"

"Sure. Look at this." She responded with a couple of soft-shoe steps suggesting barely a slight limp.

"Wait here a second while I park my car. Then I'll escort you to the trauma center over there." He pointed almost directly across the street. "They'll give you a quick look to make sure you're okay. It's not out of the way for me, my office is in the building next door."

As a warm feeling radiated through her body, her eyes drew him in. "What a small world. That's where I work, too."

Then, as the couple waited to be seen by a nurse, they spoke casually. Luke understood that Robin Hunt was a medical technician in JIT's Department of Neurology. She had grown up in a seedy part of Palo Alto living with her mother, who had chronic health problems, and an aunt. She had never known her father who had skipped out at her birth. Her early years were spent working to help put food on the table and going to school. This situation strengthened her resolve to be a survivor. In high school she excelled academically and was able to get a scholarship for college. Years of caring for her mother had motivated her to become a nurse. However, her mother wasn't there to celebrate her receiving a nursing degree as she had passed away. Though scholastically brilliant, Robin never had time to experience a social life. She seldom dated because of a combination of factors: she was far smarter than the boys in her class and taller than them, plus she was exceedingly shy due to growing up in such an impoverished environment. Her life improved in nursing school where she blossomed, becoming more physically attractive and, with it, a growing self-confidence. But her early years had made their mark. Instead of pursuing an interest in men where no relationship seemed to be to her liking, she focused her energies on developing a challenging intellectual career. Robin explained she was a medical technician in JIT's neurology department.

After learning about her background, Luke had little to say. Although he did manage to fill in one silence by mentioning he needed to hire a clerical person for his newly formed department of neurological research.

Before leaving the hospital, the doctor reported her injuries were minor. But still feeling guilty for causing the mishap, Luke asked for her phone number to follow up on her condition.

When he called the next morning, Robin wheedled out of him the requirements needed for the position he wanted to fill. She decided to pursue the job. He promised to arrange an interview with Dr. Abbott, head of the neurology department. Two weeks later she was offered and then accepted the job. The twenty-eight-year-old could barely restrain her enthusiasm. Being part of Luke's trailblazing team sounded like the opportunity of a lifetime. By learning from his creative genius, she could be on the leading edge of developments in neurology and receive the recognition and perks that come with it.

Since working with Luke, Robin excelled in the delicate handling of an introvert like Luke. Her coddling ways seemed to bring out the best in his attitude and creativity.

This morning while waiting for Luke to show up, Robin shuffled through the notes she had made last Thursday. That was the last time the two had been together. Now she was agitated at being told to report early this morning when he hadn't bothered to inform her of what had happened to him. She was on edge because Luke was the epitome of being punctual. This was unlike him; especially when they were preparing for such a very important presentation.

In the field of neurology, Luke's brilliance was opening the eyes of scientists across the country. But outside of science, he was like a fish out of water. This genius was definitely not a people person. He had no interest in people and preferred concentrating on studying neurology rather than attending anything social. Not a conversationalist, Luke was ill at ease with others, including his marriage. Despite his idiosyncrasies, Robin liked him and loved her job. In their time together the two had worked out ground rules like picking up his Dutch Brother's coffee. Once she snuck a sip of his Aftershock brew and gagged on it.

Early in their working relationship, Robin managed to get Luke to agree to certain parameters of what he expected of her. Housecleaning and washing clothes were definitely out, and running errands had to be held to a minimum. She knew he was a handful, but her caring for him seemed to grow by the day. Although at times he seemed to be such an insufferable jerk. Luke admitted that neurology was the essence of his being, and as far as it concerned her, it meant being on call 24/7. She found the arrangement had been worth it. His demands were mostly reasonable, and she strived to gain his confidence as his organizer and a sounding board for his creativity.

Waiting for Luke to show up caused her anxiety to ratchet up further. She drummed her fingers on the top of the desk. A glance at her watch showed it was 10:10. *Golly he's never been this late without letting me know. Something has to be wrong. He's not following his rule to be at work at least fifteen minutes ahead of schedule. . . If he doesn't show up soon, I'm going to have to call him. But once he chewed the hell out of me when I did because it wasn't an emergency. Well, this is one of those times!*

Ever since the early days of working together, Robin struggled to understand him. He had such intense convictions: being an introvert, opinionated, and a man of few words, to name a few. In one of those rare moments as they were becoming acquainted, he confided about not having a normal childhood. His mother had died when he was young. Then his father was seldom home because he was a travelling evangelist who embraced religion and forcing it on his son. Being strong-willed, Luke found Christianity difficult to cope with because it required a conviction in faith. For him, facts, not faith, were the key to acceptance. If a matter could not be proven, he would not accept it. Finally, after a few years of Christian indoctrination from his father, he rebelled and stopped their meetings. This caused a breakdown in their relationship. Despite his idiosyncrasies, there was something mysterious in Luke that caused Robin to like him.

"He still hasn't shown up, huh?"

The surprise of another person in the room interrupted Robin's reverie. It was Scott Stone, the third member of their team. She was reminded that he had joined the group only a few months earlier as the temporary replacement for another neurologist who had left in a huff. Evidently that flareup occurred because Luke refused to share the algorithm needed to be entered to operate the SoulTaker.

"No," Robin said. "He promised to be here an hour ago. I can't understand what's happened to him." As she turned back to her paperwork, the glance at the clock on her desk caused her to frown. *Damn it. I don't care how he reacts. I've got to call him to find out what's going on.*

Knowing his number by heart, she punched it into her phone. After six buzzes came the unfriendly recording: "I'm not here. I'll get back to you when I can." Then the line went dead.

The abruptness of his message bothered Robin. She slammed her cell phone down in disgust. In the process it smashed the little finger on her right hand causing the nail to split. "Doggone it," she yelped. *Where in the heck are you, Luke?* There was a gnawing in the pit of her stomach. I've got to remember to keep some Pepcid tablets in my purse. She was sorry for wolfing down that second Krispy Creme on the way to work. Eating sweets was her downfall.

After taking a deep breath she thought: *Luke means well. Sometimes he just doesn't know how to show it. Once he had at least tried to carry on a personal conversation by asking how Mom was doing with her dementia. But he didn't seem genuine and he quickly changed the subject back to their project.*

At one time Luke told her he never had close friends. Said it wasn't important. He admitted his social life had been a disaster ever since his wife left him three years ago. After six years of childless marriage, she left saying she couldn't take it anymore. Robin had heard stories from Dr. Abbott.

Robin couldn't stew about Luke any longer. She decided to let their boss know. Grimacing at Scott, she uttered, "I'll be back in a minute. I've got to let Dr. Abbott know Luke promised to be here early this morning but hasn't shown up yet. Something has to be wrong."

On the way to the director's office, Robin's concern for Luke seemed to grow with each step. *There's no reason for him to not be here by now or to have called to tell me why. Hopefully Phil will know something. They always stay in close touch.*

CHAPTER FIVE

The Same Day

Phillip Abbott ran the JIT Neurology Department with an iron hand. His decisions were firm and fair. But when it came to overseeing his lab research area, things were different. Luke was his son despite being adopted. The young man was so talented, and Phil was proud of him. During the two years Luke had been on board, his projects had created an ongoing stream of revenue for the university. Now the success of his SoulTaker demonstration would signal the greatest of all of his achievements.

When Robin reached Dr. Abbott's office, she found him scrunched over a pile of papers on his desk, head in hands. The tap on his door interrupted his concentration. "Hey, Robin, what's up?"

After informing the chairman that Luke had not shown up early as he promised, Abbott's brow furrowed. "When did you last see him?"

"Last Thursday when he left work. That's four days ago," Robin replied.

"You mean he wasn't here Friday?"

"No, he said he was going for a long weekend because things were going swimmingly well. You know how he likes to use that phrase when he's upbeat and confident."

"Yeah. . Yeah," Phil scowled.

Both of them knew that one of Luke's admirable traits was his reliability. He always kept them informed of his whereabouts, especially during important times.

Phil continued, "Well, he said he needed to get away. I just don't like him taking time off when we've got such a crucial demonstration coming up." His face reddened.

"He told me he had an urgent matter to attend to." Robin knew being tight-lipped was one of Luke's traits. "Once he makes up his mind to do something, there's no discussion and no stopping him." Noting the anguish on Phil's face, she gritted her teeth, fearful their discussion might give Abbott a stroke.

"Well, something significant must have happened. There's no way he would mess this up. God, I hope he's all right. . . What about talking to his brother? Those two usually keep in touch."

"I'll do that right away."

When she backed out of his office, he added, "Keep me posted, Robin. Call me as soon as you learn anything. . . If I'm in a meeting, interrupt it."

As she started down the hall, she heard him mutter, "Jeez, oh jeez. I hope he's all right."

The next stop for Robin was Luke's office. From the upper desk drawer, she withdrew his personal phone book and copied the number for John Pope.

Then, after returning to her office and closing the door, she prepared to phone JD—the name Luke's brother preferred to be called. She knew JD only slightly. He lived in Fountain Hills, Arizona, seven hundred miles from Palo Alto. Recently he retired from the military where he had been doing intelligence work. In her two years of working for Luke, Robin had spoken to JD only a couple of times and met him once as he passed through the area. It was a surprise when she finally met him in person. The two brothers were polar opposites in appearance and personality. While Luke was withdrawn and skinny, JD was outgoing and physically fit.

Robin noticed it was after 10:45 when she tapped JD's number in her cell. Upon his answering, she said, "Mr. Pope? Er, I mean, Major Pope? This is Robin, I work with your brother."

"Well, it's colonel now."

"Oh, I'm sorry."

"I'm not. It got me a big raise." He laughed.

Robin liked his sense of humor. "Colonel, your brother didn't come to work this morning. We're working on a big project and I need to speak with him. It's not like him to be out of touch. He always keeps me informed of his whereabouts. Especially, when we're working on something so important. Do you happen to know where he could be?"

"No, I haven't spoken to him in a couple of weeks."

"Could you help me find him? I'd appreciate it. It's very important."

"I'll see what I can do. . . . Say, Robin, can you give me a little background? When was the last time you saw him?"

"When he left work Thursday evening. He told me he was taking Friday off."

"Sounds unusual to take a long weekend when you have something major in the works."

"Er. . er. . ," she said. Her stuttering made it obvious she felt uncomfortable. Robin wanted to get this conversation over. She realized JD's experience in military intelligence made him a professional questioner. With his persistence, she knew she would eventually fess up. So, she came out with it. "He said something about going to San Francisco. You know he has a tendency to never give more information than he has to."

"Yes, I know. . . Hmm. San Francisco, you say." He gave a raucous laugh. "I doubt Luke's up to staying in some posh hotel." This time the laugh was more subdued. "He's never been much for spending big bucks. Now I suppose you're going to tell me he went there to see a woman."

"I have no idea, sir."

There was a moment of silence on the other end. "I don't see Luke with a woman. But if that's the case, well good for him. I didn't think he'd have it in him."

"Sir, I don't have any idea what he's up to. He told me this in confidence and said to be ready for an early start next Monday."

JD said, "Don't you worry, Robin. This is just between us. . . Sounds like he's working on something very important."

"He is."

"Maybe the SLT, huh? You know, the SoulTaker."

There was a prolonged silence.

"Robin. Are you there?"

Her reply was hesitant. "Yes, I'm still here." She was flabbergasted. *No one knows about the SoulTaker. Well, that is except for a couple of us. That program is top secret.* Her mind raced searching for an explanation on what Luke's brother might know about this. "Sir, what do you know about SoulTaker?"

"Sorry, that just sort of slipped out. Guess we shouldn't be talking about it on the phone. I know it's confidential. . . er, I should say 'top secret.' I won't say any more about it. You should know I'm very concerned about this project. I'm sure the NSA would be, too." The National Security Agency handled intelligence for the United States Department of Defense.

Robin had to end this conversation as soon as possible. Talking about something so secret made her nervous. "I'm sorry, I've got to go," she said. "Colonel, I appreciate your offer to help find him. Let's keep each other posted if we learn anything."

Upon hanging up, Robin was shaking. *What does JD know about SoulTaker? How much has Luke shared with his brother? And this makes me wonder how much any government security agency knows about it.*

A few weeks earlier, Dr. Abbott had broached the potential security concerns of the SoulTaker with an acquaintance connected with the National Security Agency. Immediately, the agency designated this project as one requiring top-secret security clearance. The government felt it could present a national security risk if it fell into the wrong hands. As a result, the NSA decided to monitor its ongoing development. Knowledge of this project was limited to only a handful of people. As far as Robin knew, those privy to this invention were only Luke, Dr. Abbott, Scott Stone and her. Then, she recalled there was also one other person. That was Diego Reyes, Luke's previous neurology assistant.

CHAPTER SIX

The Same Day

At his home in Fountain Hills, Arizona, JD was troubled by Luke's being gone without telling anyone. Although JD was the youngest of the three brothers, Luke had been raised as the baby of the family. For as far back as JD could recall, Luke needed special attention due to a couple of physical problems: frailness and chronic asthma. Physically he was on the puny side, but mentally he was a giant. Having a brilliant mind, his focus was on intellectual issues rather than socializing. Science and math became his comfort zones. His interests combined with his high intellect made him a master of those regimens. This lifestyle meant he relied upon others to orchestrate his social life because he was often too devoted to his science projects to think about anything else. Ironically, he hated having his whereabouts monitored all the time. Fortunately, the situation improved when Robin came to work for him. She had developed a knack of respecting his privacy without causing him to be upset about her keeping tabs on him.

It wasn't a complete surprise when Robin had phoned him after not being able to find Luke. In recent conversations with his brother, JD felt his growing stress. His SoulTaker invention was a double-edged sword. While it was a terrific breakthrough for science, it brought with it the moral dilemma of invading a person's privacy. Should he complete the project or destroy it? The more the two of them discussed the matter, the more JD stressed the dangers SLT presented regarding privacy. Especially, from a security viewpoint. No person exposed to this invention could be assured their thoughts would remain confidential. Having a SoulTaker unit could be mana from heaven for anyone interested in stealing information from another person. Furthermore, the person whose mind was explored would not even be aware of what had happened. JD had suggested that Luke keep his invention secret until he shared his concern with Dr. Abbott. Hopefully, they could come up with a solution to handle the problem.

One thing was certain about his brother: When it came to dedication to his job, no one was more responsible. There had to be a damned good reason for Luke not being available when important things were developing.

Robin said she hesitated to contact Luke by his cell unless it was as a last resort because he cherished his privacy. But since he was late this morning, he should have kept in touch when he had made such a big deal about the importance of meeting early today.

As he mulled this over in his mind, JD became more concerned. His first instinct was to try and contact his brother immediately. So, after getting no answer by phone, he decided to text him. In the past, when Luke was aware JD was trying to reach him, he had always returned the call within minutes.

An hour later, after getting no response from Luke, JD figured there was a problem. He had to be involved in finding his brother. However, doing so would require taking a different tack. In the past month, JD's physical condition had worsened. He now had to operate from a wheelchair.

He had sustained a serious injury to his lower right leg and during recovery contracted sepsis. The result was an amputation of his leg six inches below the knee. Fortunately, exceptional fitness, both physical and mental, was allowing him to make excellent progress. Physical therapy had already begun and he was in the process of being fitted for a prosthesis. His positive attitude was contributing to a speedy recovery.

As far as the public was concerned, JD recently retired from the military, had returned home to where he grew up, and was operating a security business in the area. No one except his wife knew he remained in the military as an undercover agent. He had been assigned to root out terrorism on the home front. At forty years of age, he would soon be eligible for retirement due to twenty years of service. But he was too much of a patriot to call it quits when danger lurked at home.

Twelve years in the US Army combined with his exceptional skills in military intelligence had made JD a prize commodity in the fight against terrorism. Then, for the next eight years, he began the circuitous route of performing his duty on different fronts. First, he worked for the CIA in the Mideast, then the FBI within the US, and recently was assigned by NSA to fight homegrown terrorism in the country's southwest region.

Two months ago, he became stationed in Fountain Hills, a suburb of Phoenix. This was an ideal location since it was central to where action might take place and was within a territory familiar to him. The story he gave locals when he arrived was that he left the military to recover from PTSD. He announced setting up shop as a security consultant for area businesses. It was a cover that could be easily believed because it had been his home for some time and it gave him the freedom to focus on whatever the agency needed.

The tragedy of what actually happened to JD a month earlier had taken place not far away. It was at night when a series of wildfires were spotted in a heavily forested area on the Mogollon Rim ninety miles northeast of Phoenix. The pattern of forest fires suggested it could be more than a coincidence. If not controlled, the fires could merge and destroy thousands of acres of timberland. With this a possibility, the agency ordered JD to lead a team to explore causes for the fires. Upon investigation, it had the earmarks of a terrorist attack. Six attackers were discovered and four were killed in a skirmish. In the gunfight, JD's lower right leg was shattered. The wound was beyond repair. It required amputation. Two of the terrorists were captured and held for questioning at an undisclosed location. JD was to have been in charge of the operation, but his injury forced him to be put on temporary leave.

JD never told his brother about the incident, because Luke was considered the pacifist of the family. Plus, as far as Luke knew, JD was now retired. At first, having to lie to Luke about staying active in the military troubled JD because the boys had always trusted one another implicitly.

Luke managed to keep JD informed about his revolutionary invention. Both felt the SoulTaker could be a terrifying tool if it fell into the wrong hands. In fact, when they last spoke two weeks earlier, Luke said he thought of destroying the invention because of the danger it posed for mankind. He had revealed this feeling to both Phil and Robin as well. But if someday he decided to demolish it, he would just do it. Luke was confident his ingenious invention was so unique and groundbreaking in its concept that it would be years before anyone else could figure out how to do this.

JD felt his first step in trying to find his brother was to talk with Phillip Abbott. Although JD had lived with him and his wife in a foster-home relationship for a few years, Phil's attention had been largely focused on Luke. Over the years JD's connection with Phil became superficial; they kept in touch on special occasions like birthdays and holidays.

When he called Phil, JD said, "Robin called a few minutes ago to tell me she's concerned about Luke. Guess he didn't show up for work this morning when he ordered his people to come in early to work on a special project. I wonder if his absence has anything to do with the SoulTaker. I know—"

Phil interrupted him. "Just a minute JD. What do you know about the SoulTaker project?"

"I know he's worried about how his invention can affect people's privacy. Luke and I have talked about it. I agree with him on some dangers we could face if others have access to using it. Not only does it invade a person's privacy, but his system could also jeopardize our national security."

"I'm shocked Luke spoke to you about this. He's aware the government has decreed what he's working on is top secret."

"Phil, I'm every bit as concerned about top secret operations as you are. Remember I work for the U S government."

"Yeah, I know."

"Luke and I have always been close and tell each other about what we're doing. It gives us a chance to confirm the decisions we make are best. You know me well enough to understand I can keep secrets."

"Yeah, I agree. . . JD, on a related matter, I have talked to a close friend who works with national security about Luke's project. After I did, he discussed this with the NSA and they have decided to monitor the development of his invention. Hank Mitchell is the head of the agency's Western District. He's assigned to follow upon this since the invention is likely considered top-secret."

JD replied, "I'm glad we could discuss this. You can count on me to do whatever I can to help find my brother. But I do have one limitation. I have to do so from a wheelchair. A short time ago I ruined my knee in a hiking accident." That seemed more believable than mentioning he was shot in a fracas with terrorists on Arizona's Mogollon Rim.

After their conversation, JD came up with a way to help in the search for his brother. He decided to ask for assistance from someone he trusted implicitly. Immediately the name Cameron Dalton came to mind. Cameron was a longtime army friend. For years the two had worked closely together on intelligence activities. Cam was a self-starter, smart, and a conniver. Besides he owed JD a favor. The last JD knew, his friend was a private investigator who worked in the city where Luke was last seen.

CHAPTER SEVEN

The Same Day

That afternoon, a couple of hours later at the neurology lab, the anxiety over what could have happened to Luke gave Robin a splitting headache. While they were still waiting for Luke to show up, she and Scott finished preparing the SoulTaker checklist so when Luke arrived, they could proceed in preparing for the demonstration.

After Robin had finished her part, Scott continued to complete the more sophisticated part of the assembly. Although Luke kept secret the algorithm to unlock and run the system, he had made an exception by sharing it this one time with Scott. After that the code would be automatically changed, so once again Luke would be the only one who could operate it.

The current cipher to open the system had been written by Luke on the back of his PhD diploma which hung on the office wall behind his desk. It seemed ideal to have the formula easily accessible for Scott.

A while later Robin was interrupted by a tap on her door.

"I've done as much as I can," Scott said. "Now it's all ready for Luke to give his blessing."

In the recent tests of volunteers, the SoulTaker system had been functioning well. Its nonverbal communications were considered successful at a rate far greater than expected. The random vacillation in laser signals had been virtually eliminated by Luke. Thus, over ninety percent of the responses were accurately understood. And the pleasant surprise was that when the data on the patients' minds was analyzed there was significant improvement in remembering the ideas that had been implanted.

Scott continued, "I know Luke wants to handle the testing himself. But I'm ready to review some of the patient feedback. Robin, could you pull up the SLT files for me to look at?"

"Sure, be glad to."

As they went to the central computer to access the SoulTaker files, Scott asked, "How did we ever come up with the crazy name 'SoulTaker'"?

"You can thank Luke for that," Robin said. "In designing his creation, he worried that if someone with the wrong intentions gained access to the system, they could do bad things. Say, like getting confidential information they weren't entitled to. Who knows, maybe even trying to control another person's thinking. Then it would become a weapon. It'd be like stealing a person's soul. That's how he came up with the name and it seems to have stuck."

She stopped for a moment to massage the pain in her neck caused by this morning's stress, then continued, "Luke likened his invention to Pandora's Box. You might recall that Greek myth about a certain container given to Goddess Pandora. If opened, the container would release all the evils of the world. And when it was closed that kept 'Hope' trapped inside. Luke began to have second thoughts about releasing his program. He felt the dangers of misusing SoulTaker might outweigh its benefits. His solution was to attach a safety mechanism so the laser couldn't operate unless a code was first inserted. That's why he established an algorithm known only to him."

During this explanation Robin had been searching for the SoulTaker file on the lab's main computer. After entering the password, she was stunned to find all of the data was missing. "I can't believe it Scott. There's nothing here." In a state of shock she stammered, "At least we've got the prototype. Let's get it out of storage."

The prototype was the one and only device they used in their testing. It consisted of three parts: a revolver-looking laser beam, a receptacle the size of a cigarette pack, and operating controls similar to an electrical mouse, all of which could fit in a shoe box.

They rushed across the lab storage area where the device was held in one of the wall lockers. The locker was secured by a combination lock requiring inserting three numbers to open it.

Upon seeing the lock Robin said, "Oh my, I forgot. Luke is the only one who knows the combination."

"No worry," Scott replied, "when I was a kid, I learned to open these things in a heartbeat."

After a few minutes of fiddling, Scott proved he knew what he was doing. But, to Robin's surprise when he opened the door, the locker was empty. She gasped, "Oh, my god, this can't be happening. Not only are all the files gone but so is the prototype. Someone has taken everything. . . I don't understand what's happened. What have you done, Luke?"

Scott replied, "Things were fine just last Thursday. Luke and I had been running trials on patients until he left for his trip." He scratched his head as if this act might help him remember what had happened at that time. "Earlier last week we did have one situation that concerned us. It was with S-12. That volunteer was a 21-year-old grad student. She was very cooperative. Didn't feel nervous. Her concentration was good. After Luke entered the access code, he focused the laser on her cortex. The signals were good for the first ten minutes. Then suddenly her message became garbled. The scowl on her face told us she was in agony. We stopped right away. She complained of a splitting headache and just didn't look normal. So, we stopped the study and, to be safe, sent her to the trauma center for a CAT Scan and an MRI. Turns out she might have had a TIA."

"Was that the extent of any problems with those being tested?" Robin asked.

"There were only a couple of incidents. One of the volunteers reported having a memory lapse after her test. It lasted for about twenty minutes. In that case Luke managed to repair a glitch in an erratic laser beam, which resolved the problem. That's all I can think of right now...Incidentally, we did have a number of successes: One man was able to recall several places where he had lived before starting kindergarten. Another had given up smoking two years earlier, but when Luke implanted the idea of desiring a cigarette, the man lit up as soon as the interview ended. Some others couldn't remember what had happened during their testing. When we were done, Luke said he'd lock up the device and wait until continuing more fine-tuning Monday; that's today. That's the last time I saw the prototype."

"Well," said Robin, "thankfully we have another option for finding information on the missing SoulTaker. Luke always keeps a backup of all his work on his personal computer."

She scurried into his office and scrolled through his documents. Soon she called for Scott, not aware he was right behind her. "You're not going to believe this. His files are missing too. . . Jeez, Luke. When did you do this? . . . I know you made some notes on the project the other day. . . Let's see, that was last Wednesday. Two days before he went on his trip. What could he have done with it? I can't believe he'd destroy his own creation. . . He must have hidden it someplace until he decides what to do with the project. I've got to report this to Dr. Abbott."

CHAPTER EIGHT
The Same Day

It was almost noon in San Francisco, when Cameron Dalton ended his conversation with his old army buddy, JD Pope. The two had remained close for nearly twenty years since sharing time in military intelligence. JD's brother, Luke, was missing and this was a concern because the neurologist had been working on a confidential project having national security implications. This intrigued Cam and he acknowledged owing his buddy a favor.

He stared out of his office window at the San Francisco skyline. Actually, the view from his cramped third-floor office in the Mission District wasn't worth talking about. His attention was drawn to the Tanqueray Gin billboard plastered on the back of a building across the alley. It was a nagging reminder of his New Year's resolution to resist drinking until 5:00 o'clock. *God, I do need a drink.* Justifying it was that time somewhere, he slipped a flask from his bottom desk drawer and unscrewed the cap to take a swig. The swill burning down his throat signaled his attitude was about to improve.

Cam's concentration returned to thinking about his own problem. Soon he would be facing a threat from Johnnie. *How's it going to feel having the fingers on my right hand broken?* His watch read 1:52. It was less than three hours until his gambling friend at the Palace Poker Casino would decide whether to inflict the punishment he had promised.

Cam gambled regularly at Johnnie's blackjack table in the afternoons. Over the past year the two had developed a bond at the gaming table. It was against house policy, but Johnnie had extended

Cam a personal line of credit. He could borrow up to ten thousand dollars, as long as it was repaid within one week. But this privilege came at the cost of a ten percent service charge. The arrangement had been a win-win for both of them: Cam temporarily salved his gambling urge and Johnnie got some personal spending money.

Today was the deadline for Cam to pay his debt in full. He was $8,500 short of the $18,500 he had owed Johnnie. Already the dealer had extended this payment for a second week. That had never happened before.

The problem had been caused by a luscious forty-year-old client. She had skipped town leaving Cam holding the bag for $15,000 in his expenses. He had been hired to gather information on the escapades of her husband Royal Merit, a multi-millionaire. If she had her way, that guy was going to pay dearly for his philandering.

For the previous five years, Cam's PI business had been either "feast or famine." A recent big payoff hadn't lasted very long. Instead of depositing his windfall in a 401K, he bet it all on one hand of blackjack. And lost. Ever since then, he lived with the current arrangement made by Johnnie.

Their meeting could be a disaster. If Johnnie did what he promised, Cam would be nursing his pain with a neat scotch. The detective wasn't a religious person, but right now he prayed for a miracle.

Then his thoughts returned to that earlier call. "Hey, Cam how'd you like to make a buck?"

JD needed help in locating his brother. He explained the U S government was beginning a search for both Luke and his invention. Hank Mitchell of NSA was organizing efforts to track them down and it made sense for Luke's brother to bring in a detective like him in whom he had confidence and trust.

Next, he told Cam about losing his leg in a fight against terrorists. This limitation meant he'd have to operate from home. JD needed someone to be active in the field and available immediately. He offered to cover all expenses and pay him whatever fee was considered reasonable. It only took a moment for Cam to respond. He could be counted on as long as JD wired him an advance of ten thousand dollars this afternoon. His per diem would be one thousand per day. JD said he would wire the funds immediately and promised to call back very soon with an update on what the police had found about Luke in both Palo Alto and San Francisco. That was where he supposedly had a fling with a lady-of-the-night.

Less than an hour later, Luke's brother gave the detective another call. First, the money Cam requested had been wired. And second, JD had used his military connections to gain access to whatever the San Francisco police had learned. Luke's car had been found in the parking lot at the Marriott Marquis Hotel in San Francisco. The room in which he stayed had been left a mess. But the worst of the damage occurred in the bathroom where the shower door had been broken along with the porcelain sink and mirror above it. Also, traces of blood were discovered on the floor. Since the authorities felt Luke had been abducted, a forensic team had been brought in to investigate. Near the service entrance at the back of the hotel, they found a pushcart full of linens soaked with massive amounts of blood. In addition, hotel security tapes covering the lobby showed Luke entered an elevator accompanied by two men and a woman. There was a possibility that another man trailing the group might also be involved. Cam agreed to start his investigation the first thing tomorrow.

CHAPTER NINE
The Same Day

About six that evening Robin arrived home to find her roommate Maria waiting for her. Robin had called that morning to say Luke was missing and feared something bad must have happened to him. While Maria knew Luke only slightly, she was a friend of Diego Reyes, Luke's former assistant. Until four months ago Diego had worked with both Luke and Robin. In fact, Diego had been the one who convinced Robin that Maria would make a good roommate for sharing the rent.

"How are you doing, honey?" Maria asked as she came to Robin and hugged her. "Any more news on Luke?"

"Nothing. But a lot of people are looking for him. That includes the local police and the San Francisco PD. This morning I called Luke's brother, JD, to see if he knew where he might be. JD was surprised to learn he was missing. He wondered if it might have something to do with the SoulTaker. There's a possibility the SoulTaker could present a national security problem. According to JD, the government is concerned about it falling into the hands of people with bad intentions; you know, like spies. Evidently a friend of Dr. Abbott who learned about the invention brought it to the attention of the National Security Agency. They feared it could be used for espionage. Since Luke was last seen in San Francisco, authorities are checking there on the possibility he might have been kidnapped.

"I don't mean to upset you Maria, but your boyfriend might be involved. I think Diego's leaving the lab had something to do with the SoulTaker. Did he ever tell you anything about why he left?"

Maria replied hesitantly, "No. . . er, no. . . He never told me. Why?"

"I think he left 'cause he was mad at Luke."

"I know he was upset. He just never said what it was about. You know he's very outgoing, but he never talks about his work. . . Come to think about it, he grew unhappy about his relationship with Luke. Said it was over personality differences. But I can read Diego fairly well. There definitely was a problem. He keeps things to himself. Then one day he suddenly called it quits. You've worked closely with him, Robin. You know how he can be."

"I know," Robin replied, "he's an enigma. Diego's so outgoing and friendly. Then, he can switch moods abruptly and sulk. He just clams up, gives you a sour look and walks away. . . I used to kid him about his macho Hispanic genes. But he couldn't take a joke when he was in one of those moods."

Maria said, "All I know is Diego was getting awfully frustrated. He felt Luke didn't trust him anymore. Said it was not comfortable working with him."

Robin's attention returned to Luke. "I've got this bad feeling that something has happened to him. He always shows up for work as promised. Especially when he asks Scott and me to come in early. And if something ever came up, he'd certainly let me know. Well, this is a big week for us. It could be the biggest one Luke has had since coming here. Getting ready for Thursday's demo is just too crucial for him to miss." Her shoulders slumped revealing her emotion.

It was obvious to Maria that Robin needed consoling. "I know how concerned you are, Robin. The two of you have grown so close. It's like losing a brother."

Robin nodded as she wiped the tears away and blew her nose.

"Stay right there, Robin. I'm going to pour you a glass of wine. It'll make you feel better."

While Maria left, Robin reminisced. She was uncomfortable sharing her innermost feelings about her workmate. Her thoughts ran rampant. *Luke's become more than a brother for me. I really care for him. I'd do anything for him. Sometimes I get tingles when he brushes by me. There are times I just want to hold him in my arms. He's so fragile. So insecure with women. Lately he's been pulling me closer, even though it isn't romantic. His divorce had seemed like a blessing, but he's become so lonely. Living alone has to make him irritable. He needs to share with someone. But lately, he's treated me like a spouse without benefits. My duties have taken a bizarre turn. He's gotten me to oversee his housekeeping and running errands. And it's grown worse. I'm not his social agent.*

"Are you alright Robin?" Maria asked as she returned with a glass of pinot grigio.

"Yeah, sorry I got caught up in thinking about him." Until now she had managed to keep those feelings to herself. His demands had put a strain on their working relationship. She loved her job too much to risk losing it. And him as well.

"The best thing for you right now is to have this drink and try to get a good night's sleep. . . I hate to leave you alone tonight. But I have an important engagement."

After a tender touch to Robin's arm, Maria excused herself. She went to her room to make a call on her cell, then hurried to leave their apartment.

CHAPTER TEN
The Same Day

Just prior to leaving Robin, Maria had called Diego asking him to meet at their favorite place. The closeness of their relationship was something the two had worked hard to keep from others.

Maria's cryptic invitation told him she had something important to say and needed to meet as soon as possible. She realized the news concerning Luke would be important to him. Ever since he left the lab, there wasn't a day he missed quizzing her about Luke's progress on his work.

While waiting for Maria, Diego thought about being one step closer to stealing Luke's latest invention. He felt certain he already knew the news she was going to give him. What he had been working on was beginning to unfold to the public as of this morning.

He took time to think about his plan which began to evolve five months earlier when he was learning the value of the SoulTaker.

As he had worked with Luke, Diego became excited about the bizarre idea of seizing the device and selling it for a fortune. But the big impediment to the plan was getting Luke to share the algorithm needed in order to open and operate the device. Without the code the SoulTaker was useless. After weeks of frustration in failing to get Luke to share the code Diego realized he would have to resort kidnapping him and then somehow induce him to divulge the code.

Well, his scheme had worked like a dream. Luke called the exotic woman who Diego had arranged to contact. The setup seemed to be perfect and romantic. It was to take place on Valentine's weekend at the luxurious Marriott Marquis hotel in San Francisco. This happened last Friday evening.

Diego took a moment to relive how things worked out. He had stationed himself in a dark corner of the Way Station Bar next door to the Marriott hotel. Krystal Ball, Diego's floozy, was waiting for her target to show up. A few minutes after the six o'clock established rendezvous, Luke arrived, out of breath and adjusting his necktie. As he dashed by a row of tables, he stopped with a jolt to spy one of the most gorgeous women he had seen in a long time. She was within arm's reach nestled in a booth. Looking down at her, the stare from baby blue eyes accompanied by a sensuous smile told him it was her. He couldn't keep his eyes off the tight low-cut sweater which invited a long gaze. She resembled the picture sent on a text to him.

"Excuse me ma'am," he stammered, "are you Ms. Krystal Ball?"

Her subtle nod indicated he was right.

"I want to thank you for being here. And for all the trouble of arranging an evening with me. I've certainly been looking forward to it."

"Me, too. It's my pleasure Dr. Pope."

"Please call me Luke. Dr. Pope is my father."

Raising her eyebrows showed corny jokes weren't her thing. "I'll call the waiter over to order you a drink. You look like a martini man or would you prefer a Scotch on the rocks?"

"A martini sounds good. It's been a long time since I've had one."

With a snap of her fingers, the waiter was at their booth. "Rodrigues, my gentleman friend would like a martini. He'd like it dry."

In a jiffy his drink arrived in a frosted glass.

Carefully he took a sip, then downed the rest in a gulp. Noticing his tenseness ease, she flicked her finger for a refill which quickly appeared.

As they were becoming acquainted, he excused himself for a trip to the john. His weaving as he headed down the aisle seemed pronounced. Then, before returning, his date had plopped a tiny object into his glass. Shortly, Luke started slurring his words, Krystal knew it was time for her next step. Diego saw her mouth something to two humongous goons seated nearby. "He's ready. Let's get him up to my room before he passes out." A couple of minutes later, Kristen and her group were parading through the elegant Marriott Marquis. Her buddies, she called Frick and Frack, each held an arm escorting him through the lobby with his feet barely touching the ground. Diego brought up the rear of the procession.

Upon arriving at the room, the two thugs launched Luke head-over-heels onto the bed. "Holy shit," one of the monsters fumed in disgust. "Look what that A-hole did to me." His partner bellowed in delight, "He sure did a number on you." Frick's sport coat looked like it had just been retrieved from a landfill in the rainy season. Splattered puke blanketed the front of it.

Appearing white as a sheet, Luke gasped for breath. Immediately, Diego recognized the problem. He spotted Luke's luggage in the corner, jerked open a carry-on and rummaged through a daub kit until he spied a quick-relief inhaler. He slapped it on his partner's face, who after some wheezing, managed to free his airway. The attack subsided quickly.

"All right, you guys, yank off his clothes and throw him into the shower. That should sober him up," Diego ordered. "In the meantime, I'll track down a laundry cart, then we'll take him down to the service entrance. Krystal, baby, get rid of any traces that he's been here. I'll be back after I've pulled the SUV up to the loading dock and brought my Porsche around. When we leave, Krystal you can ride with me while we   escort you two and Luke to his new temporary home."

"It didn't take the thugs long to strip the clothes off their passive prey and pour him into the shower. Hit with a blast of icy water, Luke reacted with a fury. He was uncontrollable like a tenacious gorilla lashing out in all directions. In a ferocious rage he shattered the glass shower door, then dove headfirst into the porcelain sink. Blood gushed from a gash on his head spraying crimson all over the immediate area.

By the time Diego returned with the laundry cart, Krystal was on her knees sopping up the blood. She had used most of the towels as well as the bed sheets. "My God,' Diego exclaimed, "what a fucking disaster. What happened?" She explained what had transpired as she continued with the cleanup. "I'm trying the best I can, but there's too much gore all over the place."

"You've done as much as you can. There's no way we're going to cover up a crime," he said. "We've got to get out of here as fast as we can. Diego stuffed his friend's clothing in the suit bag along with his daub kit and watch. But he managed to keep his wallet. Then Diego found some scotch tape in a desk drawer which he used to bandage a washcloth over the bleeding gash on Luke's face. By that time, the two men had crammed Luke's unconscious body into a Marquis Marriott robe, rolled him in a blanket and chucked him into the laundry cart.

The vigorous shaking of Diego's arm stirred him from his reverie. Maria blurted, "Robin can't find Luke. He never showed up today. She's sure something bad has happened to him."

"Baby, is that why you had to see me right away?" he asked as she approached him in the corner booth at Lucky's Tavern. This was where the two of them sat whenever it was available. Situated as far from the bar as possible and with dim lighting, it afforded the intimate setting lovers appreciated.

When Maria plopped in next to him, she avoided reacting to the squeeze on her thigh. Instead, she glared at him and pumped out questions like a gangster with a machine gun. "What do you know about that? It's that woman, right? The one you set Luke up with on the Internet. You took him, didn't you?"

"Hey, hold on. I don't know what you're talking about," he lied.

"I'm talking about that sleazy woman you thought Luke should see. The one in San Francisco."

"Did I say that?" Diego pursed his lips. *Oh hell, that must have slipped out when we were drinking.*

"You bet. Did you have something to do with Luke's being gone?"

Slowly shaking his head, Diego could tell she knew he was lying. *How do I get out of this?* Then he said, "Sounds a little paranoid to me. Luke's old enough to take care of himself. Don't you think Robin's jumping to a lot of conclusions?"

Maria continued her attack. "Where did you get that woman, anyway?"

Diego wasn't prepared for the third degree. Maria had always seemed so demure and even keeled. He stammered for an answer that hopefully seemed plausible. "I . . . I . . er . . got her number from one of my old friends."

He wasn't going to admit that it came from Uncle Rafa. Actually, Krystal was on the cartel's payroll. Once she agreed to the job, Diego had made a point of driving to San Francisco to meet her. Immediately, he became so captivated by her beauty that he asked her out. The two had four dates in five days and Diego became smitten. They had already slept together by the time he planned to dump Maria. He had never been with someone so sensual. Krystal was there for him in every way. She loved his Porsche 911 and he let her drive it whenever she wanted. He never would have believed the things she did for the cartel on a regular basis.

Diego continued talking, trying to justify his actions by deflecting the grilling she was giving him. "Even though Luke and I had a falling out, I always considered him a friend. I'm sorry that I was such an ass. My problem was when we worked together, he kept so much of the SoulTaker development to himself. It was like he didn't trust me. I couldn't understand why what he did was such a secret. If I understood better what he was doing, I could have been more help. Why did he have to keep so much to himself?"

"Robin said Luke was worried his invention could invade a person's privacy and he didn't know what he could do about that. Until he figured that out, he was considering keeping his creation a secret."

"Well, I wish he would have shared his thoughts with me," Diego replied. "He is still my friend. Please let Robin know that I'm here to do whatever I can to find him. . . In the meantime, Baby, we should be figuring out how to spend more time together. I sure love you. Hope you can come over to my place soon."

Diego breathed a sigh of relief when Maria said goodbye. She had left in definitely a better frame of mind than when she arrived. *God am I good. I think she still trusts me.*

Thinking of the fairer sex caused him to reflect on Krystal. He had to see her soon. And he knew she felt the same because she was expecting another five grand—the second half of the cash promised for helping to abduct Luke. The beating Luke suffered hadn't seemed to bother her at all. She certainly was a tough cookie for someone appearing so sweet and naïve.

With Luke's kidnapping completed, Diego figured what remained to be accomplished would be relatively simple. All he needed now was to swipe the SoulTaker prototype from the locker at the neurology lab. Then with Luke and that apparatus in hand he would make Luke give him the code to operate it.

The following day Cam luxuriated in his office celebrating his good fortune. He pondered yesterday's situation as he swirled the ice in his Tanqueray with his stockinged feet propped comfortably on the top of his desk. Things had gone well, and he relished returning to his carefree lifestyle.

Within two hours after yesterday morning's phone call from JD, the promised ten thousand dollars had arrived in his bank account enabling him to personally deliver it to Johnnie. Cam met Johnnie's deadline which allowed him to leave their meeting with his hands intact. But the rules of their arrangement had changed forever. Cam would no longer be given a line of credit. And in a way that wasn't all bad, because he was now forced to do a better job of controlling his gambling urge.

Now at 5:30 in the afternoon, he phoned JD to report on the assignments he had been given. "Hey, JD, it's been a good day. I appreciate the speedy delivery of the money. This morning I met with the San Francisco PD. Detective Sgt. Mackey couldn't have been more accommodating when I mentioned your name. He gave me the files related to your brother's presumed abduction and promised to keep me informed of any new developments."

"Were they able to confirm if the blood type found in the hotel room was my brother's?"

"Yeah, it was, and there was a hell of a lot of it. Mostly in the bathroom. Chances are he survived the attack. But he had to be damned weak by the time he left the place. Forensics suggested he could well have needed a transfusion and more than likely he experienced a concussion. A piece of his scalp was left behind. He shattered the shower door and put a crack in the porcelain sink. After that he was taken to the hotel's delivery area in a laundry cart."

JD commented, "The manager of security services mentioned he showed you a tape of two vehicles that were probably involved in the abduction: A black Toyota SUV and a gold Porsche 911. They found Luke's Camaro in the hotel parking ramp."

"JD, a camera in the Marriott lobby showed Luke was escorted to the elevators Friday night, shortly after seven. Two enormous men built like NFL football players swept him along arm in arm. And following them was a well-built blonde. There also might have been one more in the group. A skinny Hispanic guy with a ponytail got into the elevator at the same time. Then about an hour later another security camera caught some of those people at a rear loading area in the back of the hotel. It showed the two big guys stuffing something huge into a black SUV. The laundry cart left behind was empty except for plenty of traces of blood. When the SUV left, it followed the Porsche out of the area. That was driven by the woman who escorted Luke through the lobby. And guess what, that guy with the ponytail was riding with her. I did see the California plate on the Porsche. It was one word, "Appaloosa." I'm checking with the California MVD to determine the owner.

In the morning, I'll head to Palo Alto. I plan to follow up with the police there and also Dr. Abbott."

"You'll have to keep NSA informed, too. Hank Mitchell is the agent in charge of coordinating the investigation. Dr. Abbott will tell him you're working with me. You also need to check out Luke's apartment. I'll make sure the landlady lets you in. She's already taken the police through the place. Things seemed to be a little messed up. Let me know if you find anything unusual in your inspection. Otherwise, I'll talk with you tomorrow."

CHAPTER TWELVE

February 18

Shortly before noon the next day, Cam visited Dr. Abbott at his office in the neurology building at Jobs Institute of Technology on the Palo Alto campus. Also attending the meeting was Hank Mitchell of NSA. After Cam reported what he had learned from the San Francisco PD and the Marriott Marquis Hotel, Agent Mitchell mentioned that a related search was also underway. This was for the SLT prototype which was missing from its locker in the neurology lab. It wasn't certain whether Luke had done something with it or possibly it was taken by whoever took Luke. Mitchell asked Cam to regularly report his progress since NSA would be coordinating both investigations.

It was about one o'clock when Cam went to the nearby neurology lab to meet with Robin and Scott Stone. Cam had arranged this appointment yesterday afternoon. During their discussion, the detective came to understand the intricacies of the SLT and that Luke was the only one to fully control the system. He learned about Luke's concern that the SoulTaker afforded too much power for anyone to have and thus he considered destroying the system rather than allowing it to fall into the wrong hands. It presented both moral and ethical issues. Based on her working closely with Luke, Robin guessed he might have put the device in a safe place until he decided whether he would continue its development or destroy it.

After gulping down a burger, fries and Coke, Cam visited Luke's apartment which was close to the JIT campus. He was optimistic about discovering something to help in his search for both Luke and the SLT.

Maggie O'Keefe, Luke's landlady, fretted about what the police had done to Luke's place. She complained about having to take time to bring some order back to his apartment. Cam experienced her Irish temper when she warned him to not cause another mess. She didn't have the time because she was in a hurry to visit her sick mother who needed attention. Fortunately, Maggie mellowed as she spoke about her tenant. Luke was quiet, kept his room neat and never complained. Using all the suaveness Cam could muster caused her to sympathize with Luke's situation. By the time she was ready to leave, he had convinced her to let him have whatever time was needed. He promised to leave the key to the flat in her mailbox when he was done.

By early evening the detective was dog-tired from a hectic day. It had been some time since he had to work so hard. He had gotten up at nine a.m. in a stupor, driven to Palo Alto, had back-to-back meetings, and was now frustrated after several hours of searching Luke's tiny apartment with nothing to show for it. In disgust, Cam slammed his hand against the top of the desk causing a piece of paper to sail to the floor. This caused him to think. *The hell with it. It's time to call it quits. Any more searching is nothing but a waste of time.* Uttering a groan, he dropped to his knees and picked up the sheet of paper. *It must have been hidden on the underside of the drawer.* The paper was speckled with scribbles that made no sense. But after further examination he figured they were symbols handwritten in cryptic fashion. He counted twenty-six letters and numbers, presented in groups of five:

dxxym ylnpu ofnmf nhyyx siolc x

He smiled, realizing it was some sort of code. Solving things like this was one of his specialties. One thing Cam and JD had in common was expertise in encryption. For several years a major part of their work in military intelligence had been spent deciphering. Knowing JD so well, Cam remembered the two brothers grew up communicating in codes. *It's not going to take long to decipher this message. More than likely it's some sort of military code. At least this seems like a good starting point to understanding what it says.*

One of the simplest and most widely known encryption techniques was called "Caesar's Cipher." It is a substitution of ciphers where each letter in the message is replaced by a letter some fixed number of positions down the alphabet. If for example, in a left shift of 3, the letter D would be replaced by A, E would become B, and so forth. This method was named after Julius Caesar, who used it in his personal correspondence. Knowing this shift is one of the more popular techniques for encrypting, Cam decided to use this technique. The key to solving such a code depended upon determining the number of letters in the shift and whether the shift was to the left or to the right. In less than an hour, Cam had the solution. The message was easily decipherable when using the "right shift of 6" technique. The result converted the letters: 'jddes ertva ultsl tneed youri d' to: 'jddesertvaultsltneedyourid'. Then with proper spacing the message read 'jd desert vault slt need your id'.

"Fantastic," Cam muttered, pounding his fist on the desk in celebration.

That's saying the SLT is stored in a place known as "desert vault." Cam's pulse raced. After some googling, he discovered an institution located in Palo Alto called "Desert Vault, LLC." *This has to be where something valuable is hidden!* Visions of wealth and power danced in his head as he tapped that phone number on his cell.

"Good evening, this is Desert Vault. May I help you?"

"Good evening. Do you provide lock box service?"

"We certainly do."

"I'm trying to contact the place where my brother stores valuables. Can you tell me if I have access to his box? My brother's name is Luke Pope."

"Please give me a minute to check, sir. What's your name?"

"JD Pope."

"That's the initials J and D?"

"Okay, please hold." A moment later, he said, "Sorry, your name is not listed."

Cam's heart skipped a beat. *How can that be? This message must mean JD has access.*

"Sir . . . er sir. . . please excuse me. Do you have a given name? Maybe it's listed that way."

"Silly. That was silly of me. I should have given you my full name. It's John David . . . John David Pope. *Quit talking, you idiot*, Cam cautioned himself. *If I ramble on too much, he'll think I'm lying.*

A moment later came the reply. "Yes, Luke Pope has authorized you to have access to his box. To enter all you have to do is present three official proofs of identity. Like a driver's license, passport, voter's ID, birth certificate, or some other official document."

"Huh." *Three? Isn't two enough?* Cam wondered.

The receptionist seemed to have read his mind. "It used to be two forms of identity were sufficient. But we've had problems lately. So, we upped the requirement to three."

"Ugh," Cam moaned to himself, realizing this was becoming more of a pain in the ass than he first thought. "I understand. You can't be too careful. . . Say, what are your business hours tomorrow?"

"Eight until five."

"Thanks, I plan to see you then."

After ending the call, Cam had an ironic thought: *Well, as long as I need forms of identity, getting a third one doesn't matter that much. Then his stomach churned. God, the problem is I need documents and I need them in a fucking hurry. Who can help me?* Cam churned through his memory for the best source for a rush job. *Harry Lavelle. Harry used to prepare counterfeit documents on a moment's notice. But I need to get this done before JD or anyone else discovers where the prototype might be hidden.*

It had been a long and exhausting day for Cam. He was as dead-tired as any time he could remember. What he needed was the boost he could get from a couple of martinis. But he had to be sharp and efficient. Fortunately, his adrenalin was on overdrive. His mind raced. *How could I be so lucky. If I do this right, I could make a shit-pot full of money. . . or more. . . maybe a lot more. All I need now is to have some authentic-looking forged documents. Then, I'll get my gambling buddy to make a connection for an easy sale of the prototype. He told me he's got the right contacts.* Johnnie had said once: If you've got something hot to get rid of, just see me. I've got connections. According to the people Cam had spoken with today, the sky was the limit on how much Luke's invention could bring. *I've got to move fast, before JD or the government get wind of how to track down Luke's stuff.*

But Cam still had two more things to do tonight. First, he couldn't let JD know about Luke's coded message telling where the prototype was hidden. So he forged a different coded message than the one that had floated out of the desk. Then he placed it where the original had been hidden—conspicuously showing from the underside of the desk drawer—so the landlady would think she discovered it and pass it on to JD. After doing that, Cam realized he had to move fast if he wanted to get to Desert Vault ahead of anyone else. He found Harry Lavelle's phone number in the old contact book he never let out of his sight. In response to his call came a request to leave a message.

Then, during Cam's frustration at having to leave a message, the recording was interrupted by a familiar voice. "Hey, Cam, long time, no see. How in the hell are you?"

"Getting by. Right now, I'm in a real bind. Are you still in the business of forging documents?"

"Not really."

Cam's heart skipped a beat.

Harry continued, "My new wife inherited a bundle and I'm living on easy street."

"Could you do a favor for an old friend?" Cam pleaded.

"Maybe, but it won't come cheap. What do you have in mind"?

Cam explained the need for getting three authentic-looking counterfeit credentials and he had to have them before noon tomorrow. Then, he gave the particulars of what was required.

"Jesus," Harry said, "you're asking for the world. Honey and I are heading to Tahoe in the morning. She's now the love of my life. We're celebrating our six-month anniversary. Let me give you the names of a couple of guys that might be able to help you. I'll get my list—"

Cam interrupted, "God damn it Harry! Listen, if you do this for me, I'll make it worth your while. How's two grand sound?"

There was a delay in the response, then, "Make it three in cash and I might consider it."

How in the fuck can I do that? I don't know where I could scrape that together in one day. Then it hit him. "Tell you what, you can have five grand when my deal comes through. But first I've gotta present authentic looking documents at a meeting by five tomorrow afternoon. A minute later and the deal would be off."

"Sorry, no can do," came the response.

Cam felt as though he was going to pee his pants. He pleaded, "Harry, if you do this, I'll make double that."

After a long pause, the response came. "Will you give me the cash when I give you the docs?"

"I won't get paid for a week to ten days."

Another long pause and then Harry said, "Tell you what, Cam, you've always been fair to me. I'll do it for ten grand, if I can get the cash within thirty days.

Cam gulped, then said, "Okay, we've got a deal."

After the call ended, Cam wiped perspiration from his brow. He had no choice but rationalized that if things worked as he hoped, he would be rolling in dough long before Harry's deadline. Next, he thought about contacting his gambler friend tomorrow to begin the search for a buyer of the SoulTaker. Johnnie would have an opportunity for an incredible commission if he put a big deal together. *I never realized how much fun being generous can be.*

CHAPTER THIRTEEN

February 19

It was around one o'clock the next afternoon when JD received a text from Luke's landlady. "I appreciate your man keeping Luke's apartment neat and tidy yesterday. But when I cleaned up this morning, I did find one piece of paper sticking out of Luke's desk drawer. Thought you might want to see it, so I'm attaching a picture. It makes no sense to me. Maybe it's important to you."

JD recognized the scribbling was from his brother. The two hadn't communicated this way in years, but he readily recognized a code they had used. It read: dxmfn bcxxy hchuj nwycf cha, which upon decoded read: jd slt hidden in apt ceiling. JD's initial reaction was a surprise that Cam had somehow missed it. Otherwise, he would have easily deciphered it.

JD phoned Luke's landlady back. But with no answer, he left a message asking her to see if she could find anything hidden under the ceiling tile. A short time later she texted: I can get to it soon. I'll check it out and call you back.

Half an hour later she returned his call. "I found one part of the ceiling where a tile was out of place. When I removed it and looked inside, there was nothing there. Once I got down, I did see some dust on the floor right below that area. If something was hidden there, it's gone now."

JD thanked Maggie for her trouble. Then he immediately phoned Cam to see why he hadn't noticed the debris on the floor. As thorough as he was, it seemed impossible for him to not see something so obvious.

Cam's reply to JD's question was surprising. "I've run into a problem. Just got some terrible news about my wife. She's been in a horrible accident. Her car was totaled. Don't know how bad she is. She was taken to the Zuckerberg Hospital and Trauma Center in San Francisco. So, I'm on my way to see her. Don't bother to send me a per diem. Let's just call it even. Thanks for the temporary advance. I didn't come up with anything at Luke's that could shed any light on where he might be. If I think of anything else, I'll let you know."

JD was flabbergasted by his friend's curt response. He couldn't blame him for supporting his wife. But something didn't sound right. Was this an excuse to get out of helping? Cam only seemed to be available when he needed something. *I can't help but wonder if he had another reason for getting out of helping me.* Without another thought, JD decided to wire some flowers to Cam's wife at the Trauma Center. That was the least he could do. *What was her name? Coretta? Floretta? Oh yeah, it was Corrie. Corrie Dalton.* He would order the flowers from the gift shop once the registrar gave him the room number for his wife.

Twenty minutes later JD received a text from the hospital registrar. "We are unable to locate Ms. Corrie Dalton. No one with that name has been admitted to ER today."

Although it seemed preposterous, JD wanted to verify Cam's story about his wife's accident. One way to corroborate it was to have Hank Mitchell check with the hospital. Around an hour later the NSA agent reported that Cam's wife had not been admitted to that hospital today. JD could only wonder: *What are you up to Cam?*

CHAPTER FOURTEEN
February 20

Late the next morning from his home in Fountain Hills, JD wondered if Luke could have moved the SoulTaker to a more secure place. Dr. Abbott had phoned earlier to tell him Robin reported the SoulTaker prototype as well as all related computer files were missing from the lab. So, JD decided to get the latest information directly from her. In their conversation Robin gave a detailed description of the prototype and how it was stored. She described the device as the size of a revolver plus two eight-by-ten-inch book-sized attachments. This meant everything could easily fit in a safe deposit box if he wanted to keep the SLT secure and control its whereabouts.

Then he asked if she knew about him having a safe deposit box or where he banked. As they spoke, she returned to Luke's office to retrieve his personal phone directory. Although she did not find any bank listed, she discovered a hastily scribbled entry for the phone number of Desert Vault.

As soon as the conversation with Robin ended, JD dialed the number. When his call was answered two buzzes later, he asked, "Good morning, sir. I'd like to check on renting a security box. Do you have one with dimensions of at least sixteen by eight by four inches?"

"We sure do. That rents for three-hundred dollars a year. We could fill out an application over the phone, if you like. What's your name please?"

"John David Pope."

"Sir, you have to be pulling my leg," said the receptionist.

"What do you mean?"

"You were just in here. You emptied the box and hurried out."

JD mumbled to himself, "God dammit, Cam. You beat me to it. Now you've taken off with the SLT. We'll never get that back. Jesus, how could I have been so stupid to trust you?"

CHAPTER FIFTEEN

February 21

It was a day later on Saturday, around eight in the morning, when Diego was rudely awakened from a deep sleep. He was not in a hurry to get up. He was languishing in the memory of the previous night's exploits with a sensuous female. By gently sliding his arm a few inches to the right he made contact with that same voluptuous woman. *She's still here. I'm living a dream that I hope will never end.* Sleeping with Krystal Ball had become a frequent event ever since he employed her as bait in kidnapping Luke eight days earlier. Ever since then, the affair continued to be torrid. Chrissy, he called her, was practically all he could think about.

Then, the drone of his cell phone pulled him from the comforting depths of sexual fulfillment. Reluctantly he withdrew his arm from a desired embrace and groped for the phone to quiet its incessant buzzing.

"Hullo," was Diego's chilly greeting.

"Diego? What's that noise I hear in the background?" came the reply.

Actually, the sound came from his companion's cooing as he stroked her breast.

"Oh, hi, baby, it's the TV," he added, increasing the friendliness in his voice. His body tensed and he stopped fondling his partner. He felt like he had been caught with his hand in the cookie jar.

"Sounds like you're listening to the playboy channel," Maria said.

"No way, I only watch that with you. . . What's up?"

"I wanted to bring you up to date on the latest about Luke. You know that invention of his, that SoulTaker thing you're always interested in. Well, Robin says it disappeared. Evidently someone took it. Robin and Scott haven't been able to find it ever since Luke's been gone."

No shit! His body strained as his focus suddenly changed. "Are you saying somebody took it out of Luke's locker in the lab?"

"I guess so."

"Jee-sus Christ. How could that be?"

"That's what Robin wonders. I haven't had a chance to tell you about this, since you haven't answered any of my messages."

"Sorry, baby, I've been awfully busy. When did she say they missed it?"

"Let's see, I think it was the day after I saw you. . . Yeah, that's right. Robin mentioned it to me when she came home from work Tuesday."

And you never let me know, did you Maria? . . . Jesus, I guess I can't blame you. That's my fault. That's what I get for being holed up in bed with my little cookie most of this week. . . Shit! Oh, shit. Now I'm going to have a hell of a time tracking that down.

In continuing her account, Maria added, "Robin thinks Luke did something with it before he went on his trip to San Francisco. That makes sense to me, because she told me he's the only one who knows how to use it. Besides, like she said before, he was having second thoughts about letting the public learn about it. He told her he'd rather destroy it than let it fall into the wrong hands."

God, he couldn't do that, Diego thought. *Certainly, Luke wouldn't have taken it with him to San Francisco. It's too valuable to leave unprotected. There's no way he would have left it in his car in the Marriott parking ramp.*

"Oh yeah," Maria said, interrupting his thinking. "There's a lot more to the story. Yesterday Robin learned from Luke's brother what happened to the device."

Diego recalled knowing JD when he worked closely with Luke. She now had his full attention. "What about JD?"

"A friend of his has it," she replied.

"A friend of Luke's?"

"No, you're not listening. A friend of JD's has it. The darned SoulTaker."

"I don't understand. How does a friend of JD's fit in the picture?" Diego asked.

"JD was determined to help find his brother. But due to a bad accident he became disabled. One of his legs had to be amputated. That meant he needed help to search for Luke. So, he called in an old friend. That person's a detective. Well, anyway, this guy Cameron Something-or-other discovered Luke had taken the device out of the neurology lab and hid it in a safe deposit box at some private vault. When JD found this out yesterday, he called that vault to confirm Luke had a box there. You're not going to believe what happened. The company couldn't understand why he was inquiring. The representative told him, "You must have a short memory. We let you into that box less than an hour ago. You cleaned it out and closed the account." Luke's brother realized someone had impersonated him by using forged documents. When JD found this out, he tried to contact his friend, but couldn't reach him. It didn't take long for him to figure out that his friend was the impersonator. He's taken the device and skipped."

So distraught by the story, Diego could not speak. He could only shake his head in amazement. Finally, he mumbled to himself, "What a crafty fucker."

Maria continued, "Robin said that JD's even more concerned about his brother now. He's calling in whatever resources he can for help."

This ratcheted up Diego's attention. He knew JD had once worked for the military but thought he had retired. Having government intelligence active in the search for Luke was going to increase his competition to find the SoulTaker prototype.

He tuned back in on Maria's comments. "So now the government is involved."

"What do you mean?"

"Robin says a National Security agent has already been assigned and is giving this top priority. Luke's invention is believed to be too valuable for state security."

Diego's gut got a little tighter. He would now have to play hardball with the big boys. His strategy had to change. No longer could he simply slip into the neurology lab and steal the prototype. He would have to locate JD's detective friend and somehow take the prize from him. *I've got to do this before the whole fucking army does.*

Immediately he knew what he had to do. It would start by getting more details from Luke's brother.

In a flash, Diego was out of bed and headed to his desk for a pen and paper. Along the way he hopped like a drunken kangaroo, staggering as he yanked on his boxer shorts.

"Maria, can you get me JD's cell number? I want to help find Luke. You know he and I have had our differences, but still, I want to help do whatever I can to find him. There must be something I can do." Diego figured that might sound reasonable to Maria. What he really had in mind was to get information from JD to track down Cameron.

"Robin's got Luke's contacts on her personal computer. Since it's the weekend, she's home right now. Give me a minute and I'll get that number for you."

While Diego was on hold his mind raced struggling to figure how he could get JD to divulge anything else about Cameron.

Within a couple of minutes Maria returned with the cell number. Before ending the call, Diego asked, "Did Robin happen to mention the name of that vault company where Luke had left the device?"

"Yeah, she had said it was called Desert Vault. Located here in Palo Alto."

"Thanks, baby, I'll give JD a call and offer to help any way I can."

Diego was so ecstatic he raced to his bed to celebrate by pouncing on the new love of his life. This happened so suddenly he forgot to click off his call with Maria. It would not have mattered if she had terminated the call on her end. But she hadn't. Instead, she overheard Diego's celebration. "Chrissy, you helped me get Luke. Now once I get his invention, I'm gonna show my appreciation. You'll get a brand-new Porsche for every day of the week and each one will be crammed so full of cash you won't be able to shut the doors. Then we're going cruising in the Mediterranean."

Diego had to move fast. His pulse was racing. Getting the SoulTaker device was now his top priority. Once he had both it and Luke, he would be on his way to collecting more money than he could have ever imagined.

As he retrieved his cell phone, he noticed he had forgotten to end his call from Maria. *God, I'm such a klutz. If I can't learn how to hang up, someday that could bite me in the ass.* How little did he know his prophecy had just happened.

When he tapped in JD's number, it was answered promptly. "Hello, I'm trying to reach Luke's brother. This is one of his former associates Diego Reyes."

"Hello Diego. Yes, I remember you. Luke called you the dashing one. You're the inquisitive Hispanic with a million questions. You kept him on his toes."

"Well, I don't know about being dashing. But he sure managed to teach me a lot. He's the most brilliant guy I've ever known."

JD said, "His regard for your talent was mutual. It's too bad you had a falling out."

"That's why I'm calling," said Diego. "Leaving him was a big mistake for me. I want you to know, I hold him in the highest regard. If there is any way I can help find him, I'll certainly do it. His ingenuity is an incredible gift to science."

"That's nice of you to say. Well, if you come across anyone who hears anything that might help, don't hesitate to let me know."

Diego's chance of learning anything substantive about JD's Cameron-guy was fading fast. Then he was struck with an inspiration. He said, "What I've heard is that you've got at least one professional working for you."

"Who's that?" JD asked.

Diego was winging it now. "The detective who got you on to Desert Vault."

"Oh, you mean Cameron Dalton?"

"Yes." Diego gave himself a pat on the back. He had Cameron's last name and confirmed he was a detective.

JD said, "Your sources are good. You probably also learned he operates out of San Francisco."

"Yeah, I did," Diego lied.

"How did you find all that out?"

"From Robin. When I was at the neurology lab, I worked with her along with Luke. We still keep in touch." Another lie.

"Oh, I see."

"Well, sir," Diego said, "when you see Robin say 'hi' for me. Here's my cell number," he gave it to him, then added, "if you can think of anything, I might be able to do, please let me know."

After ending the conversation, Diego expelled a huge sigh of relief. He now felt certain who had the SoulTaker device, and that person worked out of San Francisco. While he knew there would be plenty of competition looking for Cameron Dalton, Diego had some help too. His uncle Rafa had a vast stable of helpers through his Mexican cartel.

Next, he smiled at Chrissy as he bragged about how brilliant he had been in getting the information needed. She, whose IQ seemed to be one sandwich short of a picnic, responded with a bright idea: "You know a way to contact the detective in a hurry?"

"How?"

"Find out where he lives, then give his neighbor a bunch of money to deliver a message with the promise of a big bonus if Cameron contacts you within twenty-four hours."

Diego thought: *If that happens, my plan could be simple. I'll convince him we need each other to be successful. You provide the device, and, since I have Luke, we'll use him to make it work. Cameron, all we need is to trust each other.* Doing that convincingly didn't seem to be a problem for Diego. Uncle Rafa told him, on more than one occasion, that he had been blessed with the ability to sell ice to the Eskimos.

After giving Chrissy a warm hug, he urged her to leave. He said, "Right now, I've gotta get the hell out of here. I'll keep in touch when I can."

Chapter Sixteen
The Same Day

Several minutes after ending her call with Diego, Maria was still recovering from a state of shock. *Diego's been using me all along. God that was dreadful hearing him talk to some woman. I'm sure they're sleeping together. Even more shocking was hearing him say, "Chrissy, you helped me get Luke." Good God, Diego, you have kidnapped Luke and that slut helped you. She probably talked Luke into their rendezvous in San Francisco.*

In a jealous rage Maria heaved her cell phone across the room. It shattered a family heirloom, an antique lamp, into a thousand pieces. She screamed, "God dammit, Diego. You're a fucking arrogant asshole. I hate you. I hate you!"

Rushing into the living room, she shared with Robin what she had just overheard.

"Robin, honey, you better sit down. What I've got to tell you will blow your mind," Maria said.

As her roommate sank into the sofa, Maria continued, "Your instincts were right. Diego isn't the kind of man I should be seeing. It's worse than you think. He's the one who kidnapped Luke."

With a horrified look on her face, Robin's shoulders crumpled as she collapsed like a delicate flower run over by a steam roller. Her face turned white. She was speechless.

Maria continued, "I overheard Diego bragging about it to that floozy. That Internet woman. She helped kidnap Luke."

"Oh, my God," Robin exclaimed. "We have to save him. What can we do?"

After coming to her senses, Robin realized she had to let others know that Diego had orchestrated Luke's abduction. *But it's Saturday morning. Who should I call? This is too important to sit on over the weekend.* Then an inspiration hit her. *I'll call JD. He's got the contacts and knows how to handle dangerous things.*

JD answered his cell on the first ring and Robin divulged what she had learned from Maria.

Now, less than an hour later, from her living room apartment and with Maria at her side, she took part in a conference call JD had arranged. He had brought NSA's agent Hank Mitchell and Dr. Abbott together to hear what had happened.

First, JD told them about bringing Cameron Dalton in to help with the investigation. He reported what Cam had found regarding Luke's kidnapping, proof of his being injured, and how he had been taken from the scene in a black SUV accompanied by a Porsche bearing the California license plate "Appaloosa." Then JD described how Cam discovered the location of the SoulTaker device and managed to steal it from a private vault. Now it was up to Hank to organize an effort to track him down.

Next, he asked Robin to report on what she had learned earlier this morning. She introduced her roommate Maria to Dr. Abbott, Hank, and JD. Then the two women explained how Diego organized and led Luke's kidnapping.

At this point, Hank reminded them he would be coordinating the efforts to find both Luke and the prototype. But he stressed help from the others was important; especially from Robin since she was the one who knew the most about Luke's habits and idiosyncrasies. The NSA agent suggested they continue these calls whenever anyone had anything to report.

CHAPTER SEVENTEEN
The Same Day

Directly after taking part in JD's conference call, Phillip Abbott knew what he needed to do. He had to apprise Sterling Claymore III of what was going on. Abbott was not looking forward to this discussion with CM3's CEO. Having such an arrogant and outspoken personality, Claymore's mercurial temperament would cause the head of neurology's stomach to churn. *Just play down the drama of Luke's disappearance. Tell him investigators figured there had to be some simple explanation. Don't mention a kidnapping. Pretend he fell in the shower and it caused amnesia and authorities expected to find him wandering around, not knowing where he was. For God's sake don't say a government security agency's leading the investigation and making this a national emergency.*

How Abbott was going to handle Claymore was crucial to not losing CM3's thirty-million-dollar donation as well as a lucrative joint-venture in marketing the SoulTaker. If that occurred more contributions could be lost from other ideas Luke would develop. Then this negative thinking caused him to remember a far greater concern: the possibility of losing Luke. His adopted son meant the world to him. His absence would be devastating; far more than his contributions to creating state-of-the-art neurological advances and enhancing the university's growing reputation in neurology. . . Phil stopped his negativity. He scrunched his eyes shut, took a deep breath and decided to concentrate on a situation where his input might be helpful. He had to handle the tycoon with kid gloves.

Dr. Abbott steeled himself, took a deep breath, and dialed Claymore's private cell number. With the utmost delicacy he could muster, the head of neurology explained how, by a quirk of fate, both Luke and his SoulTaker prototype were missing.

Claymore replied, "I was expecting your call, Phil." The two men had developed a mutually beneficial relationship to the point where Claymore liked to be called "Trey." To him, it had the ring of aristocracy suggesting he was the grandson of a famous war hero and a philanthropist.

Trey continued. "Scott has been keeping me informed."

Abbott gulped and thought: *The cat's out of the bag.* Then he realized, "Naturally, it slipped my mind that he's on your payroll and you were gracious enough to lend him to us when we lost our other neurologist. So, you know Luke's absence could be serious."

"Serious?" Trey replied. "Hell, Phil, this could be a national tragedy. Right?"

"Yes sir. But we're getting a handle on it. Now that you know the importance of this, you should feel reassured that the National Security Agency is heading up the investigation. I'm confident that with their expertise we'll get Luke and his prototype back very soon."

"You think so, huh. Let me tell you something, Buster. I have yet to find any government agency that doesn't have its head up its ass. . . Listen, Phil, here's what we're going to do. We're going to put my CM3 security man on this case. Dutch Schultz doesn't fuck around with a bunch of incompetents scurrying around all over the place. We've run circles around the FBI and all those other alphabet operations. You get your NSA agent to give me a call. We'll get the Luke-thing solved so fast it'll make your head swim."

The call abruptly ended. A horrified Abbott slumped over his desk wondering what had just happened.

CHAPTER EIGHTEEN

The Same Day

Shortly after Dr. Abbott concluded his distressing phone call with Sterling Claymore, Robin came to meet with him in his office. He had asked her to discuss the situation because she had good judgment and he trusted her. Maybe she'd have a suggestion on what could be done. The first thing Abbott said to her was, "We've sure got ourselves tangled up in a hell of a mess. And after speaking to CM3's CEO it's gotten even more complicated."

"How's that, Sir?" Robin asked.

"After our conference call this morning with JD and Hank Mitchell, I phoned Sterling Claymore to bring him up to date on the latest developments. He now knows Luke has been kidnapped by Diego Reyes and Cameron Dalton has stolen the SoulTaker prototype. He's also aware that the NSA will coordinate the investigation. Claymore believes bringing in NSA is a farce. As far as he's concerned, finding Luke and the SoulTaker are too important to be left to a government agency.

"What does that mean?" she asked.

"He let me know his company is going to head up the investigation."

"Huh?"

"He told me in no uncertain terms that CM3's security department is far better in handling this problem than any federal government agency. I'm not to worry about the investigation. I'm supposed to tell Mitchell he's not in charge. If Mitchell has a problem with this, he should check with his superiors. They know CM3 has the best investigative operation around. When I tell Hank about this, I'm hoping he can set that man straight."

As Robin was about to leave, Phil said, "If you come up with any ideas on what else we can be doing, give me a call. Nothing's going to be done in the lab until Luke is found. Why don't you take Monday off. That'll give you more time to think about what else we can do to find him. You know him better than anyone else does. I'll keep you posted on whatever I hear about the investigation."

On the way back to her apartment, Robin's mind began developing a plan on how she might make a contribution. There was no way Robin could sit back and hope the others would be successful in tracking down Luke and the prototype. It was apparent that of those working on the investigation she was the most knowledgeable in understanding the traits of both Luke and Diego Reyes.

First, she decided to focus on Diego because she became familiar from working with him for several months. He was smart, had an insatiable desire to succeed regardless of moral principles, and was definitely a ladies' man. But he seemed insecure when it came to comparing himself to intellectually superior people, like Luke. Although he was a cocky braggart, he made it a point to keep his private life private. Hardly anything was known about his background and family connections. One of the exceptions was the pride Diego embraced in his uncle. Calling him "Rafa," Diego had let it once slip that Rafael Perez was the brother of his mother. She had passed away when he was very young.

On this morning's conference call, JD had reported one of the cars involved in Luke's kidnapping had the California license plate "Appaloosa." That reminded Robin of something Diego had once mentioned. He had grown up working for his uncle in San Francisco at a Mexican-owned business called Appaloosa. It was in the import-export business. Robin could not forget this name because it was her favorite breed of horse.

She wondered if there were any companies in San Francisco using Appaloosa in their name. Googling for an answer, she uncovered several. Within an hour she had narrowed the search to three. Maybe, she thought, the Better Business directory of businesses might help her find the right one. She had become familiar with them a few months earlier when Abbott had asked her to see what the BBB revealed about Claymore's CM3 company.

The locations of the three "Appaloosa" businesses gave her a possible clue as to the one she was looking for. It turned out one of those three was located in a warehouse district near a wharf. This was a more likely choice for finding Diego's uncle since the other two were located in a shopping center and a strip mall which meant probably retail operations.

While Robin's Appaloosa strategy seemed to be a long shot, it gave her something to do with her time off on Monday. That was better than just sitting around worrying if the others were making progress in finding Luke. She missed him terribly. If and when she saw him, she would certainly give him a piece of her mind. *Stop chasing other women when you have your best possible choice already caring for you every day.*

CHAPTER NINETEEN
February 23

It was Monday, two days after Robin last met with Dr. Abbott, and the day he had designated as a day off, because of the search for Luke. It was time to take a trip. The clock on the dash of her Mini Cooper read 6:50 a.m. when Robin spotted a familiar site: a Dutch Brothers Coffee shop. Attempting to avoid some of the traffic, she had gotten an early start from her apartment in Palo Alto. The trip of less than forty miles to San Francisco took almost an hour. Seeing the coffee shop that had become so familiar to her had to be a good omen. It seemed unreal to find one of these establishments, because it wasn't like there was one on every corner. Stopping by such a facility had been part of her daily morning ritual. For every workday she had picked up Luke's energizer drink—the Blue Rebel drink called "Aftershock." Thinking of him brought a lump to her throat.

Faithfully following her MapQuest directions, she was drawn to a remote street where warehouses were less imposing. Soon she caught sight of a one-story building sandwiched between a couple of prominent two-story structures. It seemed like an architectural afterthought as the adjacent buildings appeared to give it support. Tacked near the front door was a hastily painted sign reading Appaloosa Enterprises. Looking at the placard Robin muttered to herself, "Bonanza. I've struck pay-dirt. The manager has to be Diego's uncle. Now, if I'm lucky, maybe he can help me find Diego."

Light emanating through a battered venetian blind in the small window next to the door suggested someone was already at work.

A shiver ran down Robin's spine as she left her car to enter the facility. *Is this place for real? It looks more like a front for some criminal operation.*

With a deep breath, she opened the door and entered the cramped office area. The space was jammed with furniture too shabby for even Goodwill to accept. It consisted of a large desk, office chair, leather sofa, a file cabinet and a small table covered with a bunch of electronic equipment. On the wall was a life-sized poster of a well-endowed senorita wearing a low-cut blouse carrying a basket of fruit. Robin smiled at the irony of a Hispanic whose melons compared favorably with those in her basket. A door behind the lady seated at a desk led to what was probably a restroom. On the desk was a name plate: Rafael Perez, Proprietor. Seeing this, Robin knew she had hit the jackpot. Perez had to be Diego's uncle.

Although some papers lying on the desk were upside down from Robin's view, a quick glance at the letterhead read: Los Lomas, in larger type, with Mazatlán, Sinaloa below in smaller print. She had seen that name before, but it didn't register at the moment.

"Good morning," Robin chimed in her friendly nature.

The petite Hispanic woman hunched over the desk gave a caustic smile showing she was in no mood for a conversation. "May I help you?"

Her tiny size emboldened Robin. "You surely can. I'm a freelance reporter writing a story about family businesses. If I write an article on your operation, it could dramatically enhance your business."

"Huh." The response was accompanied by a blank stare.

"What I meant to say is: Ma'am, this story could increase your sales and make you more money. Wouldn't that be nice?"

"I don't think so."

"My heavens, don't you want more business?"

"I don't think so. I like it quiet."

For Robin, it couldn't have been clearer. This establishment didn't want to promote its business. Possibly it was a front for some illegal activity. So, she forged ahead with a unique proposition. "You wouldn't happen to have a father and son who work together would you?"

"No," she said displaying a wary stare, "but Senor Rafa does have a nephew."

Bingo! I'm ecstatic. Robin thought. But the feeling was short-lived. For at that instant, the front door was yanked open causing her to nearly jump in the air. The bulk of a man who entered filled the entire doorway. He barked, "What's going on Sofia? What does this woman want?"

"Er . . er . . she wants to help us increase our business."

Bulky man replied, "She does, does she?"

Without missing a beat Robin said, "Good morning, Sir. I'm a reporter working on an interesting story. I'm writing an article about the transition of a business to family members."

He stared at her with a glum look on his face.

She continued, "I was hoping for a heartwarming father-son story." Nodding towards the old lady, Robin said, "She says you have a nephew working in the business with you. Is that right?" As she spoke, the tenor of her voice seemed to lose its confidence and she avoided eye contact.

"No, my nephew works elsewhere. . . Lady, you seem sort of nervous to me. I'd like to see some identification, if you don't mind."

Expecting something like this might happen, yesterday Robin had gone to the trouble of printing a personalized business card. She extracted one from her purse and offered it to Sr. Perez.

Jo'an Barnes, Freelance Reporter
7534 S. Ventura, San Rafael, CA 94901
415-726-5368
gdnews12@gmail.com

The humongous Hispanic studied the card for a while, then staring at her said, "Lady, I don't know who you are. But I'm not buying. . . Why don't you show me another ID? Let's see your driver's license."

Almost before he finished the sentence, she bolted by him and out the door. Heading for her vehicle, she nervously fumbled for the key. After diving into the tiny car, she laid rubber as if she were starting in the Indy 500.

Chapter Twenty
The Same Day

The proprietor of Appaloosa Enterprises quickly suspected the woman who just fled from his office was looking for his nephew. Rafa Perez had to contact Diego to see if he knew who she might be.

One of the first things Rafa did when they planned to kidnap Luke was to give Diego a new cell phone number for privacy. Working together to achieve their goal had strengthened their special bond. Success would result in financial independence and allow Rafa to escape the clutches of Los Lomas.

Twenty-two years earlier, when Diego was six years old, his mother had died. And since the boy had already lost his father, Rafa felt obliged to adopt the child. Diego was given special treatment because his uncle felt responsible for his bother-in-law's death. When Diego was two, his father had been killed in a shootout with another Mexican drug cartel. Over the years, as Rafa's importance in Los Lomas grew, he recognized his adopted son had the intelligence and potential to do well outside of the dangerous, dirty drug business. So, he financed Diego's college education and encouraged him to pursue a legitimate career. Diego's interest in science drew him into the field of neurology. Then, in the past year a special opportunity came about which dramatically changed their futures.

The break came when Diego was working for Luke in the research lab at JIT. What made this happening so opportune was the invention of a device that would significantly advance neurology.

The development of Luke's SoulTaker apparatus was far ahead of its time. Although it was too early to understand its full potential in interpersonal-neurological-communication, the invention presented a unique way to communicate with another person's mind. It had untold possibilities in psychology and appeared to have untold power for whoever controlled it.

Diego saw the SoulTaker's incredible value as a nefarious tool for things like mind-control, brainwashing and espionage. During conversations with his uncle, the two came up with the idea that control of this device could be worth millions of dollars. But to do so, they needed to find someone who had virtually unlimited resources. Through the combined efforts of Los Lomas and a Medellin cartel, it seemed a sale was imminent. They had arranged a demonstration for scientists of North Korea and Iran very soon. In fact, the demo was scheduled for this coming Saturday.

With only five days to go, the uncle was getting nervous. There still remained the challenge of having Luke's memory restored in time to conduct the presentation. This reminded him to get an update on Luke's condition from the Los Pueblos Health Center. He tapped in the doctor's number.

"Good morning, Dr. Herrera, how is my patient doing?" Rafa asked.

"I'm happy to say we're making progress. You can rest assured he will be sufficiently recovered within the next week. I realize you've been pressing me to hurry up the process. But when you consider what his condition was when you dropped him off, I would say his recovery borders on being miraculous."

Rafa said, "We brought you into this because of your reputation, Doctor. And I'm paying you a hell of a lot of money. I know you're doing all you can. But we're running out of time. He has to be cured by Friday. That's in four days. You've got no choice. He must be lucid by then. Do you understand?"

"You've made the deadline very clear. And we're doing everything we can to make that possible. Er . . . er . . . because your deadline seems absolute, there could be a way to possibly hasten the recovery. I could—"

"Do it. Just do whatever it takes. Time is of the essence."

"I've never used this before. But there is an experimental concoction that's supposed to speed up recovery in situations like this. It contains adrenalin and is thought to have minimal, if any, negative effects."

"Well, use it Doc. Keep me posted. Gotta go right now."

The vibration in his cell phone indicated Rafa's expected call was waiting. He answered.

"Senor Perez, this is Mahdi. I'm calling to report everything is on schedule on my end. I'm checking to confirm you are set for this Saturday. Now what's the time and place?" Mahdi Shivani was the middleman who represented the Iranian-North Korean consortium.

As soon as the arrangements were agreed upon, Rafa tapped in Diego's special cell phone number. His nephew answered on the first buzz. "What's up uncle?"

"I wanted to let you know I had a special visit this morning. A reporter. Asking questions about my family. Said she wanted to do a story on us. What a fucking line she had. I'm sure what she really wanted was to find you."

"Was she tall, with short dark hair and big boobs?"

"That's her."

"She worked with me and Luke at the lab. Didn't take her long to connect us, did it?"

Rafa replied, "Once she knew I suspected her of not being on the level, she vamoosed. I'll bet the authorities will be keeping an eye on me to see if I can lead them to you."

"I'm sure glad you gave me this new cell. They'll have a hell of a time tracking me down."

"How's it going in your search for that maldito (damn) laser device?"

"I'll have it real soon. But I know we'll have to cut this detective in on the deal. I've just made contact with one of his people and expect to see him soon. I'm sure he knows we have to join forces to make this happen. Don't worry Uncle, I'll get it worked out."

"Listen, Diego, don't be greedy. Give him whatever he wants to make him a partner. There isn't enough time in our lifetimes to spend all the money we're gonna make on this deal," he said with a guffaw. "Buena suerte (good luck). Remember only five days to payday. Nos vemos luego (See you later)."

On Tuesday, the following morning at 9:15 a.m., Robin was seated across from Dr. Abbott in his office. Seeing her knees shaking showed how anxious she was to report yesterday's good news of tracking down Diego's uncle. After recounting her visit to Appaloosa Enterprises, he said, "Well, young lady, I thought you were taking the day off to think about how we could find Luke. I never imagined you would be so active in the search. I must say you're quick-witted. You've done more on this investigation than anyone else."

With a proud smile, she replied, "At least, we've found a way to make contact with Diego. I'll bet you anything he'll be more careful now in contacting his uncle."

"Let me pass this on to Hank right away. We'll see what progress his team is making." Abbott punched in the NSA man's number, which he now knew by heart.

As yet, Hank Mitchell said his team had nothing new to report. Both Diego and Cam appeared to have gone to ground. But he appreciated learning about Diego's uncle and vowed to keep him under surveillance. That included putting a wiretap on the Appaloosa office phone.

When Robin mentioned seeing the name "Los Lomas of Mazatlán, Sinaloa" on a note pad on Perez's desk, Hank immediately recognized this entity as one of Mexico's largest cartels. It was reputedly a multi-billion-dollar operation specializing in the more expensive drugs such as cocaine and heroin. He promised to check with government authorities to determine what tentacles the cartel might have in the San Francisco area. Chances were, Rafael Perez's name would come up as being part of the Los Lomas operation.

Next, the agent said, "Dr. Abbott, you certainly have a very resourceful person on your staff. We need her to continue taking an active role in this investigation. If it's okay with you, I'd like to have her work directly with me on this undertaking. Is that all right with you?"

Beaming with pride, the head of neurology said, "That's a darned good idea." Then, he turned to his aide, "Well, young lady, what do you think?"

Her body posture grew more erect. "No one knows Luke better than me. Yes, I'd like to do it. I've got a good handle on the prototype, too. Count me in, Mr. Mitchell. When and where do I report?"

"I've set up a local office here in downtown. It's on the second floor of the Fed building, room 201. That's on South Main. Do you know where that is?"

"Yes." She knew her help could make a difference. Her fidgety body language reflected being energized.

"Good."

"When do you want me there Mr. Mitchell?"

The NSA agent replied, "I'll look forward to seeing you at one this afternoon?" Then, he added, "And one other thing, Robin, since we'll be working closely together on this, please call me Hank."

Before ending the call, Abbott turned his attention to another matter. He told Hank about the CEO of CM3's ultimatum to take over this investigation. Upon hearing this, the agent took the matter in stride saying he had received similar threats before and knew how to handle them. "I'll have a heart-to-heart conversation with Claymore directly."

Phil said nothing but thought, *I wonder if you've ever dealt with anyone as headstrong as Sterling Claymore III. Wish I could be there to listen to that discussion. The fireworks will surely be something to witness.*

After the phone call with Abbott and Hank, Robin headed to her desk to organize a few loose ends before visiting Hank and the NSA. While doing so, she became unsettled by the potential feud between Hank and Claymore.

She feared Claymore's arrogant go-it-alone attitude could obstruct the investigation. From what Scott had told her, in their short time of working together, the word "cooperation" was not in Claymore's vocabulary. It always had to be "his way or the highway." So, if cooperation wasn't possible, she wondered if there wasn't some way to establish communication on what he might be up to. *Maybe Scott and I can stay in touch. We've been getting along very well. I like and trust him. He's also given me the feeling the CEO doesn't mind doing unethical things when he has to.* She also knew Scott was devoted to working with Luke which led her to believe he might override unscrupulous orders from his boss. In fact, Scott had once intimated he would prefer working at the neurology lab full time.

Realizing Scott was probably back in his San Diego office, she gave him a buzz. He appreciated her concern about Claymore's unscrupulous attitude and felt the same way. This made it easy for them to strike a pact to exchange any information that seemed pertinent to the investigation.

In their candid conversation Robin explained to Scott how Diego Reyes and Cameron Dalton were involved in the investigation. This included her discovering Diego's uncle Rafa Perez was part of a Mexican drug cartel. And it seemed likely they kidnapped Luke to learn how the SoulTaker worked and then sell it to someone with an illegal intent. She also added how Cam had stolen the SoulTaker device from a private storage vault.

At this point Scott told Robin he planned to be meeting with Claymore soon. Once that took place, he would keep her updated.

CHAPTER TWENTY-TWO
The Same Day

Three days earlier Scott Stone had been told by Dr. Abbott that the neurology lab would be closed on Monday. When Scott mentioned this to Claymore, he was told a company plane would be sent for him so he could take part in discussions concerning Luke and the SoulTaker.

Now on Tuesday, the neurologist on loan to JIT's neurological department, met with Claymore in his executive office. In their meeting the main topic was to further understand how the SoulTaker functioned. After Scott reviewed what the invention could do, Claymore replied, "So you guys were able to do a lot more than just exchanging thought waves with the subject."

Scott replied, "Yes sir, we got feedback on whatever that subject knew. Or experienced. And have been able to implant ideas in his mind."

"Jesus Christ, Scott, that's incredible. It sounds like you could convince a person to do whatever you want him to do."

"Possibly."

"If that's the case, that damned SoulTaker is priceless. It would be one of the most powerful tools ever invented." Then a mischievous smile formed on his face as he added, "That's too much power for anyone to have. There's no way to put a price on it." *With that power the world will be mine.* Upon realizing the significance of this thought, he muttered, "I've got to have it. It must be mine."

"Sir, there's a real problem even if we do get the machine. We won't be able to activate it. Luke is the only person who knows the algorithm to make it operational. Like I said before, having the SoulTaker isn't worth anything unless you have Luke Pope to operate it."

"Son, I know you've been harping on this. But that's just too hard for me to believe. You'd think running it wouldn't be so difficult. Any neurologist worth his salt should be able to follow the operating manual."

"I wish that were the case. First of all, the instructions on how to operate it were erased from the SoulTaker files. Robin thinks Luke did that because he was having second thoughts on whether the system should ever be made public. And secondly, we've discovered Luke's brother JD Pope didn't take it. The person who did was the detective he hired to find Luke. That guy's name is Cameron Dalton."

Like a thermometer reacting to heat, the redness beginning at the base of Claymore's neck climbed to the top of his head. "God dammit, I'll just have my head of security get it back from that son-of-a-bitch. Dutch Schultz is the best in the business. His reputation in corporate security is unparalleled. He's able to run circles around other security operations throughout the country, including those of the federal government."

"Hold on. I'm going to get Dutch up here right away."

While waiting for the head of CM3's security department to join them, Claymore was informed of an urgent call.

When the call was connected, Agent Hank Mitchell introduced himself. "Mr. Claymore, I understand we may have a problem. Finding Luke Pope and his SoulTaker device is a matter of national security. My agency has been authorized to take charge of this investigation. Any assistance you can provide will be appreciated.

But I want you to know anything you plan to do must be approved in advance by me. I hope you can understand what I'm saying. You do, don't you?"

The CEO replied, "I recognize this case is very significant for the government, Agent Mitchell. It is for my company, too. You may not be aware, but we have a vested interest in Luke. The man is absolutely brilliant and creative. I'm investing millions in his research and will be partnering with the university on developing his inventions. Frankly, he's the goose who is laying golden eggs. You can rest assured there isn't anyone who is more concerned about his welfare than I am. My company has the very best team to lead the search for him. That's why we're determined to be on the forefront of the investigation. I suggest you speak with the FBI about who is best qualified to do this. The last time the Feds had a problem they couldn't solve they called my head of security and we saved their butts. We are not a Boy Scout operation. No one is better qualified. So, I suggest you stand aside and let my expert do the job. Why don't you have your people give my man, Dutch Schultz, the background. We'll handle it from there."

There was no immediate response. Then after a slightly longer than normal silence, Hank replied. "I appreciate your confidence Mr. Claymore, but it is in your best interest to hope I didn't hear that lengthy diatribe. I'd hate to see the IRS and the Securities and Exchange Commission camp on your front door waiting for you to arrive tomorrow morning. I'm asking you politely to stay out of this investigation. Please feel free to have your people contact my people with any relevant information you have on this matter. That's the extent of any help we need from you. Have a good day, Sir."

As the call ended, Scott's jaw dropped. This was the first time he ever experienced someone holding their own against the overpowering personality of this master manipulator.

"Well, Jesus Christ, that man's sure got a backbone," Claymore roared. "Don't pay any attention to him, Stone. He's just trying to protect his turf. We'll find Luke Pope and his device before the NSA can get their act together."

The young neurologist was dumbfounded by his boss's reaction.

By this time Dutch Schultz had arrived. First, Claymore explained the situation to him. Then he asked Scott to present Schultz with the highlights of what Robin had given him concerning NSA's pursuit of Diego Reyes and Cameron Dalton. At that time, Scott was excused and Dutch was asked to remain behind to talk further about his assignment.

"Please take a chair over here Dutch next to me. We need to talk. I want to impress on you the importance of this assignment." Claymore leaned close and placed his hand on the knee of the security man to emphasize the magnitude of his request.

"Dutch, we've been together for a long time. I don't think I've given you the attention you deserve."

"Trey, I have no complaints. You've always treated me well. As far as I figure, we have a great relationship. Seems like what you are asking me to do now is something very special. I won't let you down."

"You never have. And you're right, this is the most important job I've ever given you. If you manage to pull this off, there's going to be a hell of a big bonus for you." Dutch's eyes widened as big as saucers.

"I know you've become a great collector of sports cars."

"Yeah."

"Well, if you can get me that SoulTaker invention, I'm going to buy you a Ferrari F8 Tributo."

"You've got to be kidding. Are you sure want to do this? That sucker costs more than four-hundred grand and goes zero to sixty in 2.9 seconds."

"That's the one," Claymore said. "Now, Dutch, you've heard we need to capture both Luke Pope and his invention called the SoulTaker. This is your highest priority. You have carte blanche to spare no expense in completing this mission. So, get out there and do your job!

CHAPTER TWENTY-THREE
The Same Day

Cameron Dalton was a man on the run. Ever since absconding with the SoulTaker prototype from Palo Alto's Desert Vault last Friday, he had been in hiding.

At first, Cam had been overwhelmed by his success. He congratulated himself for being so devious and clever. He now had in his possession something that could be worth more money than he could ever spend. But after studying the device's operating manual, it dawned on him that what he had was useless without having Luke to make it work. No one could operate it without first inputting the algorithm.

Since JD told him that Diego had kidnapped Luke, Cam realized he and Diego needed each other. It would take the prototype Cam possessed along with Luke operating it to be successful. But how in the hell was he going to find Diego? That guy had to be on the run, too. Joining forces was the only solution. Cam prayed Diego was realizing the same thing.

Knowing the Feds would be hot on his tail, Cam asked Johnnie about a place to hole up. He couldn't stay at his apartment where he could be easily found. The detective was now back in good graces with Johnnie; especially after offering him an opportunity to share in cashing in on Luke's invention. Although initially Johnnie was reluctant to harbor a fugitive, he changed his mind when he heard that what Cam had stolen could bring unbelievable riches and he figured there had to be a way to share in the wealth.

For previous two days, Johnnie had secluded Cam at the home of a relative of his pit boss. The aunt was an eighty-year-old recluse with a vacant casita in her backyard. Together with the pit boss, the men brainstormed on the best way to turn the SoulTaker device into a fortune. Above all, they had to maintain secrecy on Cam's whereabouts. The Feds should already be trying to track him down.

The three men agreed that with so much at risk they should not make rash decisions. Approaching the pit boss's mafia-like contacts for help was too dangerous of an idea. More than likely, they would be outwitted and end up with nothing. The pit boss had heard of similar situations where that had happened.

Last night, over a second fifth of Tanqueray gin, it was concluded there would be a better chance of Diego locating Cam than vice versa. They had little to go on in tracking down Diego. Their only clue was knowing about one of the vehicles used in kidnapping Luke—the Porsche with the California plate "Appaloosa."

Cam was sure that when it became known he had stolen the prototype, Diego would stop at nothing to find him. Since it was common knowledge that Johnnie was a close friend of the detective, the dealer would be sought out in searching for Cam.

In the meantime, Cam had been building a file on Diego Reyes to assure he could be positively identified should he approach Johnnie. The detective had provided the dealer with a photo of Diego Reyes and his background information. These had been accessed from Diego's personnel file at JIT.

So, the plan was to sit tight and wait for Johnnie to be contacted by Diego. Nervously, Cam prayed that would happen soon.

CHAPTER TWENTY-FOUR
February 25

Diego Reyes smiled with delight when he thought about his new lover's suggestion of how to track down Cameron Dalton. *Find someone who knew him and pay for information on how to find him.* Chrissy's simple solution looked like it was about to work.

Yesterday Diego headed to San Francisco to begin his search for Cam. It had been easy to pin down the addresses for his office and residence. Although after that, making contact with him failed. The detective's office was locked and no one answered the phone. The next stop seemed to have more promise. Cam lived in an apartment building housing four tenants in a lower-class neighborhood. By the time Diego arrived, it was nightfall. Finding the main door to the apartments locked and after getting no response by pushing Cam's buzzer, Diego stepped away from the building to see if any lights were on in his apartment. While it was dark, there appeared to be light coming from one of his neighbors. Returning to the front entrance, he buzzed for a response from the lighted apartment, but struck out again. Diego was frustrated but would not give up. He wrote a brief note to Cam giving a phone number where he could be reached, signed his name, and put it in his mailbox. Then to cover all the bases, he realized Cam's neighbors seemed to be the best opportunity for making a connection. So, he dropped a note in each of their mailboxes. It read: Tuesday night. To the residents of 4801 Forsythe. I am Cameron Dalton's brother. I need to see him as soon as possible because our mother is on her deathbed. Here is my cell phone number: 612-356-8723. To show how important this is I am enclosing a fifty-dollar bill. The first one of you to tell me how to find Cam will receive another $450. By eight tomorrow morning I will be waiting at the café across the street.

By 7:30 the next morning Diego had planted himself at Lucky Louie's café within easy sight of the entrance to Cam's apartment. He didn't have to wait long for one of the neighbors to head his way. He observed a stoop-shouldered man hobbling across the street towards him.

The neighbor said he had not seen Cam in four days but knew the person who would surely know where to find him. It was Johnnie, a dealer at the Palace Poker Casino. And if he wasn't on duty at this hour, someone there would surely know how to contact him because Cam had mentioned Johnnie often. Less than half an hour later Diego was in the parking lot of the Palace Poker Casino.

An omen of a good day for Diego was at hand. Johnnie was at his table and seemed unusually friendly. Upon recognizing Diego, the dealer excused himself to make a phone call. When he returned, Johnnie said, "I just spoke with Cam. He's anxious to meet you."

"A couple of authorities mentioned they were looking for him. Evidently, it's common knowledge that the two of us knew each other pretty well. Last night two men came by my table asking if I knew how to find Cam. They were Feds. Showed me their credentials, then said it was urgent they speak with him about a government security matter. I told them I hadn't seen him in more than a week. All I did was give them his address and phone number. They left their cards and asked I contact them if I saw or heard from him. I promised to do so.

"Then, a couple of hours later, another man approached me looking for Cam. He was a lot more forceful. Got my manager to give me a break so he could question me. I gave him the same story. But this guy threatened me if he found I wasn't telling the truth. Said he'd be keeping an eye on me. Here's his card."

Diego read: "Dutch Schultz, Executive Director of Security for CM3, San Diego." It also showed an email address along with a couple of phone numbers—one marked 'for urgent contact.' Diego stored all the information into his cell phone.

Johnnie continued, "That's all I've got. Anyway, as I said, Cam's eager to meet with you. He'd like to do that pronto and anywhere you suggest. What shall I tell him?"

"Why don't you say, I'll be waiting for him at Lucky Louie's. That's the café across from his apartment." After looking at his watch, he added, "I should be back there by ten."

It was nearly ten-thirty as Diego waited impatiently for the man who controlled the SLT prototype to appear. Time had seemed to drag causing him to order a second cup of coffee which he didn't need. His hopes of seeing the man were dashed every time a car drove by without stopping. A glance at his watch confirmed he had been sitting there for almost thirty minutes. His adrenalin had caused the minutes to drag by like hours. From his vantage point he had a good view of the front door. *Where in the hell is he?* Then, the thoughts of uncertainty flooded out like a hole in a dam: *Does he really have the SoulTaker? Does he know he can't operate it without Luke's input? Surely, he knows he needs me to connect with Luke. I doubt he knows he's been in a coma. To build trust I'm sure he'll want to see him in person.*

Diego didn't realize it, but he had a lot more to worry about than convincing the detective to work with him. And time was drawing nigh. *Has Luke recovered from his injury? How about his memory? Rafa had been vague about Luke's health. Had the inventive neurologist recovered adequately enough from his coma and underlying amnesia to operate the SoulTaker? Can we convince him to work with us? I doubt he'll do it for money. Maybe we can somehow make him think he's doing it for a legitimate purpose?*

Suddenly a tap on his shoulder caused Diego to flinch. He was shocked back from his musing by a middle-aged bull of a man sporting a markedly-wrinkled face and a gray-flecked crewcut. *Where did this guy come from? I've been concentrating on the front door. Thought that was the only way in here.*

"Diego Reyes?" the stranger asked. "Sorry to startle you. I used the back entrance to make sure I wasn't going to be set up. My name is Cameron Dalton, the man with the gun," the detective quipped, referring to the design of the SoulTaker prototype. Offering his hand, he continued, "Great minds think alike. It'll take working together to make our mission a success."

There was something in the eyes of his new partner which made Diego immediately like him.

Diego said, "Let me tell you what's been happening. Eleven days ago, we kidnapped Luke at a hotel. When he fought to get away, he got knocked out and had a concussion. In the process he suffered some memory loss. The doctor treating him says he's making progress. Hopefully any traces of amnesia will be gone soon."

For Cam, leaning closer, and hanging on every word, the unfortunate news created a sharp pain in his gut. He asked, "So, you're sure he'll regain his memory?"

"The doctor thinks so according to what I'm told. Now the challenge will be to get Luke to trust us enough to show how the SoulTaker works. Then we'll have him demonstrate the device to a group of scientists who represent the buyers. If we pull this off, we'll get one hell of a big bundle. I'm thinking it'll be in the millions."

Cam's eyes bulged at the audacity of the objective.

Luke's former assistant continued, "But time is becoming a critical factor. We only have four days to accomplish this because the date for the presentation has been set. And, even more urgent is the fact that the buyers' funds will remain available in an offshore account only until next Monday. . . at the absolute latest. We'll get more specifics as the time draws near. With millions at stake, they want to play this close to the vest. I won't know the location of where the demo will take place until a day or so before. By then the doctor at the care center will have assured us Luke has regained his memory. Then, it's up to us to keep him safe until his performance." Diego guffawed at the absurdity of his statement.

During his account, Diego marveled at the attention given by his new partner. As the plan was being presented, he noticed the detective leaning forward to concentrate on every detail and nod his approval.

Once Diego completed his explanation, Cam said, "I'm impressed. It seems like you've thought of everything."

"I've been working on this for some time. We've been able to make international connections in negotiating the sale. That'll give us a much larger payoff."

Cam said, "I had been struggling to figure out how to find a buyer with that kind of money. Now with that handled we still have one major concern. We have to do this in a way where we can trust each other."

"I've given that some thought. I see two things that can help the trust issue. Throughout this entire mission, you should control the prototype and operating manual. By keeping them in your possession, it ensures your cooperation is needed to make the plan work. Then by seeing Luke you'll know he's available to show us how the system works. . . Cam, this is such a big deal, we have to do whatever we can to not screw it up. Even though we've just met, I have a concern that needs to be addressed. Please excuse me for being personal, but I've heard you might have a drinking problem."

"Huh? Yeah, I've been known to tip a few now and then."

"Well, could you hold off drinking for just a few days until we complete this mission?"

Cam gulped and gave his new partner a steely-eyed glare. "Yeah, sure kid. You can count on me to not screw anything up." With that, he smiled and held out his hand to confirm the deal.

Diego continued, "If things go as planned, Luke will perform his demonstration for the foreign buyers this Saturday. So, we need to get moving right away. The first thing to do is to take you to see Luke. He's being kept at a care center not far from here. As I understand it, he's becoming more lucid. He's still confined under mild sedation."

At this time Diego's attention was drawn to the attaché case Cam had placed on the vacant chair next to their table. Pointing to it, he said, "I presume that's the famous SoulTaker."

"You're right. I'm sure you want to see it." Cam placed the briefcase in front of Diego and flipped open the lid to reveal a revolver-looking device along with several gadgets. The case also included a notebook containing the SoulTaker operating manual plus another box.

Diego took a cursory glance through the items. 'It looks great. Seems like everything's in order." He smiled, closed the case, and give it a tender tap as if idolizing its precious contents.

As Diego did so, Cam released a deep breath. *Thank God he didn't examine the laser gun that thoroughly. Because if he did, he would have noticed one part is missing.* For Cam, trust was not in his vocabulary. *If he thinks he can cut me out by stealing this equipment, he's sadly mistaken.* In studying the owners' manual, Cam learned that of all the components comprising the device, one part was absolutely essential to its functioning. This was the computer chip lodged in the guts of the revolver. Without this part, the mechanism could not be turned on. The chip housed the electronic code system which required inputting the proper sequence of numbers needed for the laser to work. *Just wait until he tries using it.*

Cam kept the computer chip in a safe place. Being so tiny, it was inconspicuous when hidden in the money belt he wore day and night.

"I've made plans for where we can stay tonight after you see Luke."

Cam's grin confirmed how pleased he was at being a part of this incredible money-making opportunity. "Everything sounds good. Let's get this show on the road."

CHAPTER TWENTY-FIVE

The Same Day

For Diego and Cam much of the drive from Lucky Louie's café to visit Luke seemed like being at a meeting of the mutual admiration society. In less than an hour they would be at the Los Pueblos Health Center. Thus far each had told how they accomplished their missions—Diego kidnapping Luke and Cam stealing the SoulTaker prototype. The exchange led to their spirits being high. In less than a week they would be multi-millionaires. They fantasized about their dreams.

During a lull in their conversation Diego phoned Rafa to report what had been happening. "Things are going well," he started, "and thanks to this secure connection, we can finally talk without fear of anyone listening in."

"Don't count on that," was the reply. "This deal is too big to chance being overheard. Remember when I tried to cut out the Medellin cartel on a big deal. They had bugged our phones. It ruined our plans to score big on that opium deal."

Rafa didn't know it, but CM3's security team headed by Dutch Schultz had managed to tap his phone to learn what they were up to. This included knowing Diego's secret number. As a result, they were aware of the specifics on Luke's kidnapping, that he was now being held somewhere in the San Francisco area and they were planning to sell the SoulTaker to foreign investors. But, as of the moment, they didn't know the date and site of the demo.

"I understand," Diego's enthusiasm dropped a notch. "Well, I can tell you, I've got the whole enchilada and we're on the way to check on our man."

"Magnifico," said the uncle. "When you see lynchpin, our contact will give you instructions. It has all the details you'll need. Hang in there, Son, you're doing great. See you soon at the Fiesta."

Upon ending the call, Diego explained the cryptic conversation. "That was my uncle Rafa. He's helping to coordinate the operation. At the care center we'll see the doctor who's been treating Luke. When we're with him, he'll pass on to me a message that will give the specifics of where to take Luke for safekeeping and the location of the demo. Our job will be to coax Luke to help on the demo. The key part is his giving me the algorithm needed to open the SoulTaker. Even if he doesn't want to help in the demonstration, I'm sure I can operate the system once he gives me the access code."

As they neared the health center the landscape transitioned to a rural setting. Diego was captivated by the picturesque rolling hills and trees. Although he had reduced his speed to compensate for the winding lane, when encountering a sharp corner, he veered onto the center of the road. He narrowly missed sideswiping an oncoming utility truck causing it to swerve off the road.

Cam panicked, "Holy mother of god, that was sure close."

Diego replied, "Not to worry. That's the end of our excitement for the day. From now on it'll be smooth sailing."

Diego had no idea how wrong he could be.

After arriving at the Los Pueblos Health Center, Diego and Cam were immediately hustled by a flustered aide to Dr. Herrera's office. Along the way they passed two nurses racing through the halls frantically opening and slamming doors as if their lives depended on finding something.

When the doctor's door was thrust open, the aide found him doubled over in excruciating agony. The grayish pallor on his face suggested he was suffering miserably. Ironically, he was feeling worse than he looked because of losing his most important possession: The special-care patient for which he was being paid a small fortune to keep hidden.

Upon seeing the two intruders, the doctor experienced a sharp pain in his gut. Immediately he recognized the young man with the ponytail. He was the one accompanying Luke when he was brought in on a stretcher in such a mangled condition; along with a bribe and a threat if good care was not provided.

It was obvious by Herrera's look of fear that his life could be in danger. He stammered, "Lu- Luke Pope's ga--gone. It just happened. They came in to tell me only a minute ago. He's got to be around here someplace. We've been checking on him on a regular basis. God, half the time he was here he was passed out. There's no way he was well enough to walk out of here."

Mr. Ponytail blurted out, "Damned you doctor. You'd better find him right now. Otherwise, you're going to be in a hell of a lot of trouble. I hate to think what the cartel will do to you. Maybe your family, too."

Turning to Cam, Diego said, "God, we're in a shitload of trouble. If we don't find him, we can kiss our millions goodbye. But worse than that, our lives may not be worth a plug nickel."

His partner gulped at the surprise. "You're saying we could be killed? We'd better get out there and help find him."

"No shit! And we've got to do it in a hurry."

At this point the doctor took an envelope from his desk and presented it to the young man. "I've been expecting you. Señor Perez gave me a message for you."

Upon receiving the envelope, Diego said, "I don't understand how your patient could escape. I thought he was recovering from a coma and was too weak to get around."

The aide interrupted, "You're correct. There was only one time I saw him out of bed. He had collapsed on the floor. It took two of us to just get him back in bed. Since then, he's seemed so frail we haven't been concerned about him trying that again."

"Could someone have sneaked in here and taken him away?"

"That's impossible," the doctor replied. "The only way into this place is through the front entrance. This facility is not that big. Besides, one of our people is usually at the nurse's station. And the only other exit is locked from the inside. Right now, I need your help. As weak as he is, he can't have gone far. Why don't you guys start by checking the grounds?"

Jamming Rafa's message in his pocket, Diego and Cam took off to search outside.

After several minutes of feverishly combing the premises, the two men found themselves back at the front entrance. Panting, Diego said, "Guess we'd better expand our search. Let's start with that trail into the woods."

Nearly half an hour later with no success, the pair collapsed on a bench by the winding road that had brought them to the care center. Diego pulled his uncle's message from his pocket, which he shared with his partner.

"Hoping our man in good health. Good news, demo advanced to Friday. Ten am at 2106 Segundo. Key behind shutter. Two rooms ready for you at Casa Adobe under the name of Jose Lopez. RP."

"Boy is my uncle going to be pissed when he learns Luke's gone. Let's go back inside and see if anyone has had better luck in the search."

When the distraught doctor learned they also failed to find his missing patient, he said, "Well, I guess I'd better call the police."

Diego replied, "You may not know it, but your patient is a national security risk. The last thing you want to do is bring the feds in on this."

In a tone of remorse, Herrera said, "Well, under the circumstances, I guess the best thing I can do is notify Sr. Perez."

Diego replied, "That's a good idea. You can also tell him his nephew will be calling soon." The nephew was not looking forward to that.

Chapter Twenty-Six
The Same Day

The patient in Room 458 had no idea where he was, how long he had been there, or for that matter who he was. He could not remember one thing. But gradually bits and pieces of his memory began to return. The trauma he experienced five days earlier had caused amnesia.

Eventually Luke Pope would be told about the incident that took place last Friday. He could not remember that his plans for a romantic weekend in San Francisco had been ruined by someone he thought was a friend. He had been set up on a blind date to kidnap him and steal his invention. In a cold shower recovering from being drugged, Luke had fought with two abductors and in the struggle his head struck a sink causing a concussion and a long gash requiring sixteen inches of stitches. Fortunately, he was delivered to a nursing home where he received excellent medical care during his recuperation.

After a couple of days of trying to regain consciousness, Luke had his first inkling of becoming aware. It began with a sound echoing like a siren in the distance. Was something really there or was it his imagination? The bewildering noise grew in strength, accompanied by fleeting images. This disruption reminded him of a 1920s movie with the projector out-of-sync, causing a flashing of disjointed black-and-white clips. His head throbbed and he felt confused. It made no sense. Then visions evolved into unrecognizable objects raining from the sky. When closing his eyes to stop the discomfort, he realized they were already closed. *All right, take a deep breath. Try to relax.* That brought the onslaught to a crawl. But the images continued to appear. Four letters kept repeating, appearing in random order: A, C, G, T. The color of each letter remained the same: A green, C blue, G black, and T red. The varying sequences reminded him of children's building blocks, but what's the significance? Slowly they faded away. *My God, this is crazy. I've never experienced anything like this before. Will the dull ache in my head ever go away? Take another deep breath. Try to relax. There has to be some logic here. Everything feels foreign. What's happening to me? And who am I anyway?*

No answers came to mind.

Finally, by concentrating, he forced one eyelid open into a squint to see if what was happening was real. But he was either blind or in total darkness. He wiggled his toes while lying down. Flexing muscles in his lower back caused him to feel like he had been stuffed into a sardine tin.

When he raised his hand to touch his face, the stubble told him he hadn't shaved for several days. His lack of hygiene was out of character for him. Personal cleanliness had always been a priority. Using his fingers, he explored his head further to find a thin ridge running from his right temple down to his jaw. *Have I had surgery? Was I in an accident?* Next, he discovered a rubbery cap covering part of his shaved head.

His discoveries had drained him of energy. He was fatigued and frustrated. Gradually, like slipping into a warm bath, he felt enveloped in comfort.

*   *   *

A few days earlier at the Los Pueblos Health Center, a doctor and nurse continued their conversation regarding the new resident. As they approached his room for a daily exam, the nurse said, "You know we're overdue for an audit by the state board of health. This patient really shouldn't be here. He can't be more than forty and has no life-threatening issues. Besides, we don't know his name or his medical history. We've got to get him out of here."

Dr. Herrera agreed, but this was an exceptional case. At first, the doctor had balked at taking care of him, but twenty thousand in cash and the promise of another twenty thousand upon discharge convinced him to cooperate. The doctor's examination revealed that the patient suffered from a grade 3 concussion, amnesia and moderate persistent asthma. Now, a few days later, the patient's health had been improving remarkably.

In reply to the nurse's grumbling, Herrera scolded her. "Don't complain, Rosa. You're getting paid extra to care for him. So, keep quiet. And remember, if he's healthy when they pick him up, you'll get a bonus. That's a heck of a good deal, right?"

Rosa cast a gloomy look in his direction. "Yeah, but I don't like it."

He didn't like it either. Reflecting back, Herrera had felt uncomfortable with the circumstances ever since admitting the patient. He didn't like the idea of the care center's administrator ordering him to care for someone who shouldn't be here and whose identity was a secret. He recalled how the mysterious person had been delivered late at night in a bloody and severely beaten condition. Two rough-looking men carried him in on a stretcher. They were accompanied by a young man with a ponytail who presented a stack of crisp one-hundred-dollar bills along with the promise for more when the patient was released. Then, Mr. Ponytail warned, "Take good care of this man. If you don't, you'll make Senor Perez very unhappy."

As soon as the three men left, the doctor rushed to the window to write down the license plate numbers of the two delivery vehicles. One was an SUV and the other a Porsche. The SUV slipped away too fast for its license plate to be seen. But he managed to copy down the one for the Porsche. It had a California plate with just the word "Appalooza."

Next, he called in Nicky, his emergency nurse, to help care for the mangled mess of a man. Their new arrival wore only one piece of clothing—a luxurious terrycloth robe emblazoned with the emblem of the Marquis Marriott. The clothing was drenched with blood. Their first duty was to give him a transfusion since his blood level was dangerously low. Afterwards the nurse sutured his face and the result compared favorably with that of a plastic surgeon. Then they moved the newest resident into Room 458, the most remote private room in the facility.

On the following Monday morning, Herrera did some investigating. From the California Department of Motor Vehicles, he discovered the "Appalooza" license plate belonged to Appalooza Enterprises, a San Francisco business managed by Rafael Perez. One of the DMV people mentioned hearing a rumor that this import-export business might be a front for Los Lomas, a Mazatlán drug cartel. Hearing this sent a shiver down the doctor's spine and caused him to give the new patient his undying attention. Undying. A poor word choice, he thought.

Now, as the doctor and nurse approached Room 458, the mystery guest overheard the approaching conversation grow louder. *Was help on the way?*

Just outside his door, he overheard a woman questioning a man, who sounded defensive and mildly irritated. The patient held his breath and strained to listen. He didn't want to miss a word.

"He's been here far too long," the woman said. "Can't you get him out of here?"

"I sure want to. First, I have to examine him. He's bound to be coming to from that last injection. If he's making good progress, maybe he can be moved. But, in his condition, that may not happen for a few days. It also depends on when they want to pick him up."

Hey you guys. Pick me up, for what? What's wrong with me? I feel sort of normal. But maybe a little too relaxed. So, what's going on? Am I a prisoner? Where am I? And what's my name? Who the hell am I?

As the door swooshed open, his body tensed. A blinding shaft of light bounced off the far wall.

Here they come. God, what should I to do? Should I let them know I'm awake or should I play dead? . . . Dead, I think.

He kept his eyes shut as someone picked up his wrist to check his pulse. Hopefully his subtle flinch didn't reveal he was conscious. *Do they think I'm still out cold?*

"Well, Doc, what do you think?"

"He's sleeping like a baby. He's had an amazing recovery."

His head was raised and turned gently from one side to side. He felt tugging at the covering on his head, then realized they were removing some sort of bandage.

As the doctor carefully uncovered the patient's face, he focused on the stitching expertise of his emergency nurse. "Look at that wound. It's healing quite nicely. Nicky did a heck of a job on those sutures, didn't she?" The swelling had gone down in the long scar running from above the patient's right temple to below his jaw line. Since the stitches had been removed, the disfigurement was barely noticeable.

A shadow across the patient's face accompanied by a whiff of lavender perfume told him the woman had moved closer to check on the nurse's handiwork.

"So, you think we can get him out of here in a couple of days?"

"Definitely. I'll call Rafa and give him the good news."

Listen, you guys, if I had the energy, I'd jump up and run out of here myself.

The doctor issued instructions for his continued care. "After the IV-feeding this afternoon, give him another dose to keep him tranquil. The Symbicort has been working fine on his asthma. Be sure to monitor that as well. I don't want to jeopardize his good recovery."

Asthma? You mean I've got more than one problem?

The patient remained quiet and motionless until his two visitors left. Once he was certain they were gone, it required a supreme effort to sit up in bed. Several minutes later after failing to roll over onto his side, he abandoned the idea. He felt like a hibernating bear awakening from a winter's sleep. What he needed now was some more rest to regain his strength.

Sometime later when the patient awakened, he tried to focus on learning something about himself. But he still could not recall his name, where he was or why. He only knew that he had been drifting in and out of consciousness. And the pain in his head was excruciating. Resting in near darkness seemed to sharpen his other senses, especially his sense of smell. The medicinal scent throughout the room confirmed he was in a medical facility. He recalled snippets of conversation he had overheard. It gave him the feeling he was being held against his will. *Why? What have I done wrong?*

Until he learned more, he decided it would be better to not reveal he was recovering. Slivers of memory were beginning to join together like pieces in a jigsaw puzzle. He took a few deep breaths to calm his thoughts, as he struggled to figure out what anyone could possibly want from him.

If he was being held hostage, was it for money or information? Did he possess something of value? Could it be linked to those four letters of the alphabet that had been bombarding his brain: A, C, G, and T. *What was their significance?* In an inspiration he realized they were the key to neurology, the building blocks of DNA. *I can't explain it, but they have to be really important to me.* It would have been too far-fetched to realize he was responsible for inventing a laser technology that would turn science fiction into reality.

The intervals when Luke could think rationally were becoming more frequent. Slowly, the fog shrouding his brain was lifting. From nothingness, he became aware of light. As his eyelids fluttered, he was reintroduced to the distress of brightness striking the optic nerves at the back of his eyes. Along with that discomfort, he felt a caress of cool air on his shoulders and arms. Despite his contentment he desperately needed to remember who he was and why he was here. But as he was surrounded by the soothing comfort of peace, his consciousness began to slip away.

As his senses reawakened, it became apparent he was being held against his will and felt the fuzziness he was experiencing must be due to drugs. He remembered a shadowy movement accompanied by an unusual aroma that was vaguely familiar. His gut told him that whoever was holding him at least had his best interests at heart. He decided to continue playing possum until he understood more of what was happening. Once he regained his strength, he would plot his escape. But that would have to wait until he regained some energy. Once again, he drifted back into semi-consciousness.

It seemed much later when Luke awoke. *How long have I been asleep? They must be keeping me drugged up. Right now, I feel well-rested.* His increase in alertness and improved energy provided the impetus to concentrate on his situation. *I've got to get out of here.* As the haze dissipated, he became motivated to pierce the veil of darkness that had been enveloping him. His first thought was a disquieting question: *What's going on?* The second was just as disturbing: Pain! The dull ache in his head which had made all the muscles in his body constrict was receding. Then a slow panic bubbled from the depths of his subconscious, firing an unmistakable signal: *Fight or flight.* This was followed by a warning from his brain: *Get up and see what's going on.*

He decided to try it. As his eyes adjusted to the darkness around him, he satisfied his curiosity by looking around. But the pain in his head limited his movement. Cautiously, he stretched his arms and legs to realize he was wearing a hospital gown and lying in a hospital bed. With supreme effort, he nudged one leg out from under a blanket and discovered he was wearing a white sock.

Every movement sapped his strength, but he eventually lifted himself onto one elbow to scan the room. In the dim light, he could see that the sheets on his bed were pulled up to his chest. The windowless room seemed rather small. It was sparsely furnished, containing only the bed and a small dresser. A bright strip of light along the floor suggested a door leading to a hallway. Then he spotted a sink and toilet by another door.

Sluggishly, he eased his legs over the side of the bed. With a muted moan, he forced himself to stand. Dizziness quickly robbed him of his balance, causing him to collapse back onto the bed. His head throbbed from pain. But with determination he got back on his feet. Finally, he slowly hobbled to the bathroom.

The lavatory was spotless. There were no personal items anywhere, nothing to give him a clue about himself. But one thing seemed certain. . . this was only a temporary place. The conscious and subconscious parts of his brain cried in unison: *It's time to get out of here!*

Leaning heavily on the sink, Luke turned on the water and splashed his face to clear his thoughts. Raising his eyes to the mirror, he was shocked at what he saw. A bald head with bloodshot eyes and whiskered stubbles stared back at him. The shock caused his knees to buckle. *Who the hell is that?* Placing his left hand on his wet face, touching the mirror with his right hand, he anxiously held his breath. The realization hit him hard. *My God, this really is me! I can't believe how terrible I look.*

Upon closer inspection, he noticed what appeared to be a fresh scar on the right side of his head. It ran from above his ear down to his jawline. A tender exploration of the bandaged area above the scar confirmed this was the source of his pain. *What happened? How did I get here? And just where the hell is here?*

As he pulled his hand back, he noticed an identification band on his right wrist. He read:

Los Pueblos Health Center
Patient: 1385
Admitting Physician: Dr. Jesus Herrera
Allergies: None Known

Why didn't they give me a name? What's that all about? My God... who am I? I can't remember!

Rummaging through the nearby chest of drawers he found a Citizens wristwatch in the top drawer. Not particularly expensive, but practical. The time registered 6:40. *Is that A.M. or P.M.?* On a hunch he picked it up to see if anything was inscribed on the back. He found an etched design. *I know that's something I should recognize, but I can't place it at the moment. There's also an engraved message: "Congrats, Phil."* Who the heck is Phil?

Suddenly he recalled the symbol on the back of the wristwatch. *It was an icon for a DNA molecule and the engraving must have meant the watch was a gift from somebody close to him for a special occasion. Phil had to be a special friend. Could he be my father?*

Then a flash of recall struck him. *No that's not right.* Luke's exploration had been exhausting. But pieces of the puzzle burst forth like a torrent through a hole in a dam. *Phil took care of me later. He was my foster father. Matthew was my father. A minister. I literally saw more of him on TV because that was where he did his preaching.* Images continued flooding back. *I must have been about ten or eleven. When he was home, we spent most evenings sitting around the kitchen table reading "the good book." That's what he called it. He wanted me to follow in his footsteps. After a while he could tell I lost interest in our sessions. The crux of the problem was we approached religion from different points of view. I couldn't accept everything that the Bible was telling me. It's an interesting story, but to be a Christian you have to have faith. I can't do that. My beliefs have to be based on facts. Dad wanted me to approach religion with an open mind. But faith is not factual. That was too big of a hurdle for me to overcome. My attitude frustrated him and it ruined our relationship.*

But the interesting thing the Bible study did for Luke was to help him direct his career path. It led him to a search for 'the soul.' Not the biblical soul, but the soul from a scientific perspective. This led to his interest in neurology.

Luke's thoughts tumbled restlessly as he began to think about his mother. *Ginny was what she liked to be called. Actually, her name was Virginia, but for some unknown reason she didn't like it. Mom was a stunning beauty. Extremely outgoing. She loved to be involved with lots of social activities. Still, she cared for us kids. We were the most important things in her life. She was always there for me and my two brothers. I was the middle one. She called me her favorite, but being the diplomat she was, I'm sure she said that to each of us. She showered me with special treatment, especially when she nursed me through many bouts of asthma. Once she stayed all night with me in the hospital because she was so worried about my struggle to breathe. I'll never forget how she went to pieces when she learned my older brother Mark had been killed in a motorcycle accident. Sadly, a rare blood disease cut Mom's life short when I was eight. For a couple of years after that, my younger brother John and I were cared for by a live-in nurse because Dad was gone so often. Then the saving grace for us was becoming close to Uncle Phil. He became our father figure. Phil and his family lived next door as we grew up. He became especially close to me and was the one who encouraged me to go to med school. Our bond became so steadfast that I eventually joined him in work.*

The reminiscing buoyed Luke's hope to recover.

Next, he turned and searched the other two drawers of the chest. The only item in the second drawer was a set of hospital scrubs. The bottom drawer was empty.

Then his attention was drawn to a closed door. Upon opening it and flipping on the light switch, he found a nearly empty closet. All it contained was a sports coat, a pair of shoes, and a leather bag for carrying a suit. His searching through the jacket revealed nothing except a label from a men's store in Palo Alto. *Could that be where I live?* He smiled upon discovering the camel-hair sports coat and impeccably polished loafers which also seemed pricey. Once he put on those shoes, he knew he would be ready to escape. But before he slid them on, something told him to search inside the right shoe. In doing so the insole slipped out and to his astonishment he discovered a dollar bill neatly folded in half. *How could that be? I must have hidden it there. Maybe I was hiding this for an emergency. Well, I sure as hell have one now.* Then, even more of a surprise happened when he unfolded the bill. His eyes bulged upon discovering it was one-hundred dollars. *How about that. Sort of ironic, isn't it? I've got money and nowhere to go.*

For Luke, that was the end of finding anything else in the room of a personal nature. No pictures, no keys, no wallet, nothing. He twisted and pulled off the wrist band and put it on the chest of drawers.

Why am I being kept here? Money, power, knowledge? I must not be destitute having such an expensive sports coat and shoes. All I'm sure of is that the label in the sports coat tells me that I have a connection to Palo Alto. Do I live there? Struggling for an answer had given him a headache. He couldn't even be sure if this was where he was now. He was greatly distressed by the situation. One thing was certain. His gut was telling him: *I'm a prisoner here. I've got to get out right away. But first, I need an escape plan.*

There was nothing else in the room. However, at least he had come up with the first step in his escape plan. He could change into these clothes and melt into a crowd.

He cracked open the door to the hall and peeked in each direction. To his left the hall ran for about forty feet, before taking a right. Voices from that direction confirmed his belief that the corridor went by a nurses' station. To the right, the hall was much longer. But in that direction, he spotted something important. An "Exit" sign with an arrowed pointed to the right. *I've got to get out of here as fast as I can. Somebody could be checking on me any minute. Forget about changing clothes. There's no time to dress up properly.* With that, he grabbed the hospital scrubs, pulled them on, and jammed his feet into the loafers. Then he dashed from the room and hurried down the corridor. His heartbeat raced with each step in the effort to escape. Forty feet to go, then twenty, ten, now six, . . . one! Reaching the door, and without thinking, he pushed on the crossbar. A shrill blast exploded in his ears. The piercing noise assaulted him, causing him to crumple against the wall where he froze in panic. *Shit.*

Behind him, he heard shouts rushing towards him from what had to be a nurse's station, behind him and around the corner. Terrified, his eyes caught sight of a door. It was located directly across from the "Exit" door and was marked "Custodial." It was unlocked. He went in, collapsed against the other side of the door, then held his breath. He had no idea of what the consequences might be from fleeing this place, but he was sure the penalty for failing to escape would include some sort of restraint against further attempts. This was his first and likely only chance to escape.

The voices down the hall diminished. *Thank God.* Turning on the light, he saw a cramped little room jam-packed with cleaning supplies. Next to some shelves were mops, a bucket and a lightweight jacket hanging on a hook. *Son of a bitch, I forgot my sports coat. I don't dare go back for it.* Trying on the jacket, he discovered it to be a few sizes too small. The coat was so tight he could barely zip it up and the sleeves were far too short. *Not exactly what you'd see in GQ Magazine. Too bad . . . it'll have to do.* To cover his face, he plopped on a "Giants" baseball cap, a few sizes too large. At least it was big enough to not aggravate his throbbing head. His wry smile accompanied the thought of looking like a scarecrow.

With a false sense of bravado, he strode out of the custodian's room and purposefully headed down the hall towards the nurses' station. He braced for a confrontation. But no one was around in the hallway. So, with one hand blocking his face, he slinked by a nurse at a desk concentrating on her duties. He hustled to the exit a few yards away.

Once outside the complex, the sunlight was so intense he had to use both hands to shield his eyes. It took all of his composure to maintain an aura of normalcy rather than the urge to flee. He paused for a moment to take a deep breath of fresh air—freedom. But escape had come at a cost—a new wave of dizziness overcame him. As soon as he scampered around the corner, he crumpled against the building to rest and try to clear his mind.

Luke's escape could not have been more opportune. He had slipped out of the Los Pueblos Health Center unnoticed. This took place a few minutes before Diego and Cam had arrived to see him.

CHAPTER TWENTY-SEVEN

The Same Day

Help was about to come for the man who had just escaped from the sanitarium.

Not knowing where he was, deflated his exhilaration of freedom. *Where am I? Where am I going?* In this exhausted state, it took him several minutes to stagger into the nearby woods, out of sight from the care center where he had been imprisoned. Then, after several minutes accompanied with a surge of adrenalin, Luke managed to stumble through the forest until he encountered a narrow asphalt road. At this point, the isolation was refreshing. For the first time he felt safe.

On the other side of the road, he spotted a large metal cubicle offering him a place to rest. Painted on the side of this gray box in blazing yellow letters was a sign: Property of PG&E. Stay Clear! Leaning against the structure he slid to the ground with a groan of relief and remained in a seated position. Within a few moments his breathing returned to normal, giving him a chance to regather his senses. *Where do I go now?*

A moment later, a PG&E van approached at a crawl. The driver spotted him and shouted, "Hey . . . Einstein. Can't you read?"

In his confusion, the scruffy fugitive asked, "Me?"

"Yes, you. If you can't read, why don't you go back up north and join your other bums? You guys aren't supposed to be messing with my property."

The dazed man pulled himself up and backed away from the gray box. As he turned toward it, he noticed the bold warning emblazoned in bright yellow. He said, "Sorry sir, I didn't see it."

"Well, I don't want to have to come back here later to do a cleanup 'cause you decided to urinate all over our equipment. Now beat it." Field Agent Ed Kent was not in a charitable mood.

"I . . . I . . . don't know where to go."

Geez, thought Kent. *These guys are like a disease. Once the first one finds refuge, it won't be long before I have them all over the place. So far, I've been lucky. I thought this was too far south of their stomping grounds. This isn't a good place for them to do their begging.* Then the look on the drifter's face softened revealing his attitude had mellowed. *Damn, something about this guy makes me feel sorry for him. This is the last place in the world for him to be.* "Get in" he said reluctantly, although he knew that doing so was a clear violation of company policy. He motioned to him, saying, "I'll take you back to town and drop you off."

The homeless man opened the passenger door, pulled himself in and sat meekly without saying a word. He avoided eye contact.

Suddenly as Kent was pulling back onto the road, his truck was nearly broadsided by an oncoming car that was obviously out of control. "Jesus!" he yelled and honked his horn. The reply came back from the sedan in the form of an extended arm flipping him off. It was ironic that neither Kent nor his rider realized they had been nearly broadsided by Diego who was hell-bent on rushing to the health center holding Luke.

Kent studied his new passenger with guarded curiosity. The rider had a shaved head, a scroungy beard and a nasty scar on the right side of his head. He wore an ill-fitting jacket, odd-looking pants and a baseball cap far too large for his head. The attire underscored his homelessness. It was not surprising that he seemed spacey and confused; probably due to a nasty drug habit or an all-night drinking binge. However, unlike many vagrants, this one had better manners. He did not stink and had even managed to slur an apologetic "sorry sir" when Kent caught his eye. What odd behavior. It reminded him of these tragic times when so many potentially productive individuals fell prey to drugs and alcohol. What had happened to this one?

"We only have a short ride to town. What's your name?"

"I ... I ... I don't know," was the reply. Then Luke buried his face in his hands.

Despite seeing how upset the rider was, Kent pressed the issue, "You don't know your own name?"

After a lengthy wait, Luke blurted, "I'm so confused right now. I can't get my thoughts together. You see this bad cut on the side of my face. I don't know how it got there. Maybe that's why I can't remember anything. . . Where are you taking me?" There was a hint of fright in the question, as well as in his eyes.

CHAPTER TWENTY-EIGHT
The Same Day

At age 63, Special Agent Hank Mitchell was too tired of playing games to take part in another chase, especially one tracking down someone with a far-out science fiction device. Fortunately, he had told his superiors that this was his last rodeo. Thirty-five years of work with the FBI, the CIA and these past three with the NSA was more than he had ever bargained for, even if it was for the good of his country. In a way he hated to see his last assignment spent on a crackpot Buck Rogers mission. Why wasn't he given a chance to track down some Osama bin Laden terrorist and end his career with a blaze of glory. That's what he had asked his boss. The reply was a polite "no way, your heart could never survive that. Besides, if your grandkids ever knew what you actually achieved in your career, it would blow their minds." *Anyway, in another sixty days I'll retire with honor. Then I can settle in Phoenix to rake rocks at a condo and play golf for the remainder of my days.*

The reminiscing was interrupted by a buzz on his cell. With a smirk, he recognized the caller: JD Pope. J*esus, that guy is such a pain in the ass. I haven't known him a week and he's already on the top of my list. There ought to be a limit on him calling every hour to see if anything new was happening. Why does my J. Edgar demand that I cater to his every wish? This Pope guy's sure got a hell of a lot of pull with somebody higher-up.* Hank answered his phone reluctantly. "Yes, Colonel, what's up?"

"You're doing one heck of a job, Hank. And bringing in Robin to work directly with you was brilliant."

Hank congratulated himself on that decision. Thanks to her ingenuity NSA had established a connection between Diego and his uncle at Appaloosa Enterprises. The NSA agent was now able to monitor activity. Just a short time ago he learned that Diego's cell phone had been traced to a clinic called the Los Pueblos Health Center on the southeast side of San Francisco. When he reported this to JD, Luke's brother asked, "Do you have any idea how far away that is from you?'

Hank replied, "Forty minutes, depending on the traffic. I'm heading out right away and taking Robin with me. I'll have my interrogators there as well. Soon as anything breaks, I'll let you know." Then he promptly hung up.

Five minutes later, JD called again. "Hey, Hank, he got away. For some reason the manager of that health center must have given Diego the word, because he and another guy split the scene like their pants were on fire. Evidently someone there has been caring for Luke and keeping him prisoner."

"We're on it right away. Roger, ten four." Hank smiled as he ended the call with lingo he hadn't used in a coon's age.

CHAPTER TWENTY-NINE
The Same Day

The events of the nearly two weeks since being kidnapped, was a period Luke could never have conceived in his wildest imagination. Losing all sense of time, he had no idea how long it had been since he was abducted. Like pieces of a puzzle, tidbits of reality were beginning to fall into place. While he was no closer to knowing who he was, he did know where he was at this moment. A less than desirable section of San Francisco frequented by vagrants.

Luke's recollection of who he was began to emerge. *The brain is the most complex organ in the body. It's made up of billions of nerve cells called neurons as well as other kinds of cells. Why do I know that? I know this as a fact, I'm certain. Still, I cannot remember one other thing that happened before I escaped that place. This has to be a sign my memory is coming back.*

He reflected on what had happened as he was about to be dropped off by the PG&E driver. Kent had said, "In this area, there are three shelters for the homeless. You can stay in one of these for a day or so while you get your act together. Each one is run by a religious group and all have rules to follow in order to stay. You can get a meal and a warm place to sleep, but they all require you stay for a sermon after the dinner. There's a Catholic one, one's for Presbyterians and the other is non-denominational. Do you care where I leave you off?"

"No," was the reply.

"Okay, I'll drop you off at the Catholic one. It's run by Father Joseph. He's a good man. It's none of my business, but how did you end up like this? Drugs? Alcohol? Gambling? Women?" *Ha*, Kent thought, *now that's something I can understand.*

Luke rubbed his temples and then fidgeted with the cut on his head. He mumbled, "I don't remember. I don't remember my name. I don't remember where I live. I don't remember how I got this cut on my head. And I don't remember how I got to where you picked me up."

"Jesus, there's only so much I can do for you," the driver said sympathetically. "Speaking of Jesus, here we are. That's Father Joseph's homeless shelter there. I'm going to drop you off right in front. Just go in and tell them you need help. Maybe they'll let you stay until you dry out a bit." When he stopped to let his passenger out, he cautioned, "Like I said, Father Joseph is a good man. If I hear you gave him any trouble, I'll come looking for you. . . whoever you are."

"No, sir, I won't be any trouble. Thanks for all you've done for me."

"You're welcome. Now hop on out. Don't tell anyone I gave you a ride. And for God's sake, you and your friends stay out of my territory."

After a moment of studying his passenger who had stepped out of the vehicle with a quizzical smile on his face, the driver's compassion overcame him, "Wait just a minute fella." Kent reached into his back pocket, withdrew his wallet, pulled out a twenty-dollar bill, and offered it to the stranger. "Here's a little something to help you out."

The rider then turned and trudged toward the shelter door.

Kent whispered to himself, "Good luck, son. You're sure going to need it."

He hesitated for a moment as he walked up the steps of *Saint Paul's Good Shepherd Center*. Then when someone from behind nudged past him and opened the door, he followed.

Seated at the front desk was a kindly looking nun. She was plump, about sixty years old with a ruddy complexion and compassionate brown eyes behind oversized glasses. "Good afternoon and God bless you," she said warmly. "I am Sister Mary Alice. All are welcome here in the Lord's house. We pray you will find peace in His presence. Let me give you some basic information and then I'll go over some very simple rules."

Luke's posture seemed to relax until she asked, "First, what is your Christian name?"

"Ah . . Ahh." *I remember everything that's happened in the last hour, but not a damned thing before that.* There was a flash in his mind. But it left as quickly as it had come. Although it left a trace of an image on the back of his skull.

"Lu . . . Lu . . .," was all his straining brain could muster.

"Well," smiling compassionately, she added, "look over there across the room where three ladies are sitting. The shorter one calls herself Lulu, so we already have one of those. The dark-haired woman next to her is Petula Clark and the Asian woman is Cher. . . Hey, we have a Cher, but we don't have a Sonny. If you don't want to use your real name, how about we call you Sonny?"

Luke rolled his eyes. *Is she making fun of me? No, she's just being nice.* "Sonny. Okay. Sure." Clearly, he would agree to anything to get this over.

"All right, Sonny, I made you a name tag. You must wear this at all times while you are here. And, my Lord, look at the time. Dinner. . . maybe you call it lunch. . . is about to be served. However, before you go into Saints' Hall to eat, you have to agree to Father

Joseph's five simple rules of the center." She tapped her finger on the table to emphasize her instructions. "First, there is to be no foul or disrespectful language. Second, there can be no violence of any sort. Third, there are absolutely no drugs or alcohol permitted on these grounds. Fourth, while you are most welcome here, you may only stay for forty-eight hours. We have to make room for all the sheep out there in need of the Good Shepherd's helping hand. And finally, since you are here for dinner, you must stay for Father Joseph's sermon that comes afterwards. Oh, the Father is such a compassionate and pious man. His sermons are so moving it is clear the Holy Spirit lives in him. Now, do you agree to the center's rules?"

"Yes," Sonny said, as he thought: *What else can I do?*

"Okay. Go into Saints' Hall and take one of the open seats."

Sonny cautiously made his way across the crowded hall, trying to ignore the sideways glances and sneers from the restless mob. *Find peace in His presence,* Sister Mary Alice had said. The only presence to be found here seemed to be a sea of angry, hungry, edgy humanity. Finally, he made it to an open seat at one table and sat down.

A calloused hand suddenly appeared in front of Sonny, startling him. "Hey there, Mister. Welcome to my table. My name is Fat Albert and this is Banny. What's yours?"

"Uh . . . uh . . . Sonny," he said as he eased out his hand which Fat Albert shook vigorously.

"We're glad to make your acquaintance." Fat Albert was a middle-aged man about forty-five, and appeared to have been nice looking at one time, but now he had a weathered face centered by sagging green eyes. Next to him was Banny, a rail-thin man with a shock of uncombed white hair and wrinkled clothes, he looked like a nutty professor straight out of central casting.

The clock struck noon and the room went eerily quiet. Sonny looked around pensively and noticed all heads were bowed. Suddenly, a voice boomed over the loudspeakers: "Bless us Oh Lord, and these thy gifts, which we are about to receive, from thy bounty, through Christ, Our Lord. Amen."

The silence was shattered by a chorus of chairs being thrust away from the tables.

"Come on, Sonny," Fat Albert blurted. "You don't want to be the last one in the line. Let's eat!"

There was little talk as a procession of humanity made its way through the buffet line, and then returned to their seats. Sonny glanced anxiously around as people started to devour their food like a pack of wolves attacking a stray lamb. His first taste caused him to realize how hungry he was. He wasn't exactly sure what it was he was eating, and no one else seemed to know, or care for that matter. It was a hot meal with a cold drink.

After Fat Albert finished, he turned to Sonny and said, "So Sonny, tell us about yourself."

Sonny was uncomfortable starting down this road again and so he said, "Maybe later. You sure look skinny, why do they call you Fat Albert?"

"Oh, I used to be fat. I used to be a lot of things. But things change." His playful manner suddenly turned serious. "It started when I was . . ." He was interrupted by the loudspeaker announcing Father Joseph's sermon. "More later. We have to listen to this."

Father Joseph strode to the elevated podium at the front of the room. Sonny was surprised by how strikingly handsome the holy man was, with a square jaw, cobalt blue eyes, and salt-and-pepper hair combed straight back from his forehead. At about 6'2" tall, he was in excellent physical condition and immediately commanded the attention of those in the room. The priest waited for complete silence. It didn't take long as the veterans of the center hushed the newcomers. Not out of any kind of reverence, more out of a desire to get this over with.

The sermon ran on for thirty minutes, covering the human heart, good deeds and caring for one another. Towards the end, as the obligatory congregation became restless, there was the inevitable shuffling of feet and scraping sounds of utensils being dragged over emptied plates. Finally, the close was at hand.

As Father Joseph noticed the crowd's growing restlessness, he increased his cadence and boomed: "For it is written in Proverbs 24:12: If you say, 'Look, we did not know this—does not he who weighs the heart perceive it? Does not he who keeps watch over your soul know it? And will he not repay all according to their deeds?'"

Suddenly, the flash in Sonny's brain was overpowering. "The soul!" he cried as he leaped from his chair. "The soul!"

"Hallelujah my son!" Howled Father Joseph as he pointed a finger at Sonny. "That is the Holy Spirit doing God's work in that man! Praise God in all His glory!"

"Sit down, Sonny," whispered Fat Albert, yanking Sonny back down in his chair. "You don't get special treatment for agreeing with him."

"No," said Sonny. "It is the soul. Something about the soul. I just don't remember what."

"Well, that's something you will need to figure out later," said Fat Albert. "Anyway, what you need to do to get along here is . . ." He paused and looked over Sonny's head, "Uh oh."

"Sonny, is it?" Father Joseph said as he approached the table from behind Sonny.

Sonny pivoted in his chair and made eye contact with the oncoming priest. "Sister Mary Alice said you went by Sonny. Is that right?"

Sonny nodded his head almost imperceptibly. Then faced forward again.

"You have a most interesting birthmark at the base of your neck," said Father Joseph.

Sonny quickly cupped his right hand and covered his neck in embarrassment.

The priest continued, "It looks like you have been . . . "

"Been kissed by an angel," Sonny finished the sentence to his own amazement.

"Why yes. Nothing to be embarrassed about, my son. It is the mark of the Lord."

"I wanna see," said Fat Albert as he half-stood from his chair and reached over to pull down Sonny's hand. "Ah ha. It looks more like ol' Sonny has got a hickey on his neck!" He laughed out loud, which caused Banny to laugh too, although he didn't know why. Banny always seemed to mimic whatever Fat Albert did.

"Sit back down and be quiet," snapped the priest. "And you are the one they call Fat Albert?"

"Yeah," came the reply.

"Yes, Father," came the reprimand.

"Sorry. Yes, Father," corrected Fat Albert. He lowered his head at the mild scolding.

"And this is Benny. He is your friend?" asked the priest.

"Banny, Father, not Benny. Yes, he is my friend. We met about two weeks ago and have stayed together ever since. In my world, it's hard to find a friend."

"There is only one world and it belongs to the Lord. Does Banny not speak for himself?"

"Not much, Father. He's had a hard life. His parents abandoned him here in the city when he was about eight and he has been in and out of trouble ever since. Mostly small crimes, but then he fell into drugs. Meth kind of fried his brain."

The compassion returned to Father Joseph. *I understand temptation Lord,* he thought, *but why must such strong vices be put in front of such weak sinners?* "How old is he?"

"He thinks he's about thirty-five, but really isn't sure," came the answer.

My God, thought the priest. "I would have thought he was fifty. Sister Mary Alice tells me you and Banny came in two nights ago. You know the rules of the center, don't you?"

"Yes, Father, we plan to leave a little later. But we wanted to stay for your sermon."

Father Joseph looked at him with a skeptical eye. "Of course. Well, there are two more shelters nearby where you might stay the night. The Presbyterian house is run by Pastor Brown and the Rescue Mission takes all denominations."

"We sort of . . . there was a . . .," Fat Albert stammered, "the truth is we aren't welcome at the Presbyterian house. There was sort of a misunderstanding with Banny."

Good heavens. "Well, you may try the Rescue Mission. Or are you not welcome there also?"

"I think we're fine there, Father."

"I came over to speak to your new friend." Turning to the newest visitor, Father Joseph said, "Sonny, I would like you to come to my office for a few minutes. Will that be alright?"

Sonny flinched in his chair, but realized there was no escape. "Sure, Father," he said.

The priest waited for the guest to stand, then pointed across the hall to where his office was. "Please follow me." Together they walked in that direction in silence.

Entering the priest's office, Sonny noticed the crucifix on the wall behind his desk. He stared at the figure of Jesus hanging in agonizing pain.

Noticing Sonny's gaze, the father asked, "Do you know our Lord and Savior?"

"I am familiar. What's different to me is to see Jesus still on the cross. I am not accustomed to that."

"This is the Catholic manner of showing our Lord. Other denominations hold a different view. But we believe it is proper to show His sufferings for our sins."

Sonny continued to stand and stare at the cross.

Father Joseph took this opportunity to give Sonny a more thorough examination. He was different from the others. The man had what looked like a long surgical scar running from beneath his baseball cap down his jaw. His jacket was obviously a couple sizes too small allowing his arms to protrude several inches and too tight to zip. His pants were like those worn by a hospital orderly. And even more incompatible were his expensive looking and highly polished shoes. The priest felt he looked ridiculous. Sensing something wasn't right with this stranger, he wanted more information. He said, "I like to find out a little about the people who visit this center." Then he asked a series of questions: What were his religious beliefs? Did he go to church? What denomination was he? The only response was a blank stare accompanied by a furrowed brow to show he understood what was being asked, but he had no answer.

"Okay, Sonny, we can talk about that later. There's just one more thing I need from you. Please stand up and take off your jacket. . . Now hold your arms straight out with your palms up."

Sonny did as he was told.

The priest's train of thought was jolted from its intended path. But first he needed to accomplish the original task. He examined Sonny's outstretched arms and found no needle marks. None. But his concern was now focused on what had been bothering him.

"Son, where did you get your clothes?"

Hearing no response, he pressed. "Now tell me the truth."

Sonny jerked his head around looking for a quick exit.

Tell me!" the priest asked with rising anger.

"I stole them, Father. I'm sorry." Sonny hung his head.

"From where?"

Sonny looked around again. There was no escape. "From the back of a uniform truck. The driver left the back door open and I took them when he wasn't looking."

Father Joseph wasn't convinced, but he knew he wasn't going to get a straight answer. Not right away. "OK. We need to talk more, but there is something I need to do. You may spend the night here."

"Thank you, Father. May I go now?"

"Yes, God bless you, my son."

Sonny eagerly left the office. When the door had closed, Father Joseph picked up the telephone. "Sister Marta, call the San Francisco PD and San Francisco General. Ask if anyone has reported a missing patient."

"Yes, Father," came the nun's nervous reply. "Is everything OK?"

"Probably. Please make the calls and report anything back to me."

Father Joseph hung up the telephone. He slid back in his chair and sighed. He knew Sonny was different, he knew he must be in trouble of some sort. What concerned him now was what he also knew from many pastoral visits. Without Sonny's jacket on, the underlying shirt matched the pants. And he knew hospital garb when he saw it.

Sonny left Father Joseph's office and looked around for the only faces he knew—Fat Albert and Banny. *Hard to find a friend,* Fat Albert had told the priest. And for better or worse, Fat Albert and Banny were all he had for the moment. But there was no sign of them. Sonny noticed Sister Mary Alice and walked towards her.

"Excuse me, Sister, but have you seen the two men that were at my table earlier?" asked Sonny.

"Hi Sonny. Yes. They had reached the two-night limit of their stay and so had to leave. They left the center a short while ago. I take it you liked Father Joseph's sermon. He asked for your name afterward and said he wanted to speak with you."

"Yes, we talked in his office," replied Sonny. Then he looked around, not sure what to do next. He had hoped Fat Albert would stick around. *Hard to find a friend.*

"You can join the group for Bible Study in the Fireside Room at two, or if you are tired you can check in at the Men's Center. Freshen up and take a rest."

"Thank you. I think I'll do that. *A rest could clear my mind. And maybe provide some answers.*

After checking in at the Men's Center, Sonny went to the communal bathroom to clean up. In the mirror above the sink, his eyes were fixated on the cut on his head and again he wondered how it got there and if it was the reason for his amnesia. *Man, you are a sight. How could I have gotten such a long gash on the side of my face? Looks like a lot of stitches were taken out recently. I'm going to need a hot shower and a shave. Maybe that'll make me feel better, and maybe that'll jog my memory and fill in some blanks. Like—who in the hell am I?* In his head, sporadic scenes began to flash in and out of his mind, but so far none of them made sense.

"Come on! Move it!" came an irritated voice behind him. "This ain't the frickin' Hilton."

Looking back in the mirror was an angry man behind him waiting to use the sink.

"Sorry," Sonny said.

He found an empty bed and laid down. With that, he closed his eyes and drifted off. But only for a moment. There was no way he could relax when he faced so much uncertainty. He had to find answers. And for the present he needed to rely on a friend. *Hell, there's only two I know right now—in fact, there's only one I can talk to and he's left. . . I've got to find him.*

With a nudge Luke awoke refreshed. It was amazing how much a little catnap could do to restore his energy. As he rose to his feet, he instinctively thrust his hands into his pants' pockets. In the process he felt some crumpled paper. Much to his surprise he discovered two pieces of paper currency—a twenty-dollar bill and a hundred. After struggling to recall where they came from, a hazy thought began to materialize. The larger bill had been hidden in one of his shoes when he had been held captive and the other was given to him by a driver who had given him a ride. That was the extent of his memory. Feeling flush with money, he considered: *Well, at least, I can buy myself one of those coffees I really crave. What was it? Some kind of energy drink. A. . a . . "Aftershock," . . yeah, that's what it is. . . Now where did that come from?*

With a goal in mind, he slipped down the hall to where a meal and a sermon were being served. There was no way he could sit through another of those sessions. So, he crept along the dimly lit portion of the corridor and eased out of Good Shepherd Center. Much to his surprise, the setting sun basked its dying rays of afternoon on his face causing him to squint as he made his way onto the street in search of his only friends in the entire world.

CHAPTER THIRTY
The Same Day

Once Luke left the Good Shepherd homeless shelter, he was filled with optimism. For the first time that he could remember, he had a mission in mind. He was going to search for Fat Albert and Banny. At least what he recalled from the past was limited to the time since his escape from the nursing home. This was a promising start. He still didn't know who he was or why he was in this situation. But unexplained flashes of events seemed to pop up randomly with increasing frequency. It was encouraging to believe things had been better for him once and soon they might return to normal. He became aware his clothes were not his normal dress when he studied the fashionable shoes he was wearing. Logic told him the ill-fitting wardrobe he now sported would be an embarrassment in his former life. The best thing he could do was to remain calm and take things one step at a time. Currently that meant focusing on finding his newfound friends.

For the longest time he meandered through streets foreign to him. As he studied the generally unfriendly faces and shabby storefronts, he felt uncomfortable in this environment. Not knowing where he was going did not seem to bother him. Life had grown simple. Certainly, this had to be far different than what he had been used to.

Shortly after four in the afternoon, he found his buddies. They were huddled with a handful of men laughing and exchanging war stories.

"Hey Sonny, I see you found us," Fat Albert shouted when he recognized him. "What a pleasant surprise. Come on over and meet your new pals. We're all in the same boat. We have to find a new homeless shelter. We've overstayed our welcome at the places around here. Tonight, we'll be spending it with the bridge group." When the others gave him a quizzical look, he explained with a smile. "No not the card game. I'm speaking about our location." He pointed to the viaduct overhead."

Everyone roared.

With his arm around the scrawniest one in the crowd, Fat Albert said, "Frank, here, is going to furnish the beans for tonight's festivity. We're still looking for a volunteer to bring the ham."

After studying the group and feeling sorry for them, Luke realized he was in a position to help out. Digging into his pocket, he withdrew two greenbacks—the twenty-dollar bill from Kent, the utility driver, and the hundred-dollar bill he had found in his shoe. Turning to Fat Albert he said, "You can count on me." As Luke offered the money to his friend who seemed to have taken charge, Fat Albert shouted, "Let's hear it for our newest member."

One of the men close by whacked him on the back so vigorously Luke felt like the wind had been knocked out of him. The others in the crowd cheered his generosity.

Tonight, will definitely be a novel experience, Luke thought. *Certainly, one for my memoirs, which right now aren't very long.*

CHAPTER THIRTY-ONE

The Same Day

When Robin tracked down Diego's uncle Rafa at his business in San Francisco last Monday, it enabled NSA to place a wiretap on his office phone. Her brave move resulted in good news. It was in place when Diego called to tell his uncle what had happened after he and Cam went yesterday to visit Luke at the San Francisco Los Pueblos Health Center. Listening in on this call enabled the Feds to find where Luke was being held and also learned Diego's new cell phone number.

It was late Wednesday afternoon when Hank and Robin drove to Los Pueblos in search of Luke. They met with Dr. Herrera and the administrative nurse Rosa Garcia. Early in the questioning the nurse, who in opting for leniency, confessed to being a party to holding Luke. This led the doctor to divulge Rafa Perez, Diego's uncle, paid them to treat the patient's concussion and secretly hold him. Neither knew anything else other than to nurse the patient back to good health and have him ready for pick up soon. Herrera reported that just a few hours ago Diego and another man came to visit Luke. But at that time, it was discovered the patient had disappeared. Both the nurse and doctor felt it was likely the patient could still be wandering around in the vicinity because of his weakened condition. His only option, if he was lucky, would have been to catch a ride to San Francisco. However, with his severe amnesia and no money or credit cards, where he could go would be limited.

Following their discussions at Los Pueblos, Robin and Hank started their search for Luke. They began in the part of San

Francisco most easily accessible to the road from the Los Pueblos health center. By late that evening without having any success, the couple decided to call it quits for the day, get hotel rooms, and have an early start tomorrow.

Early the next morning, Hank and Robin continued their search for Luke by focusing on where he could most easily get help. That meant hospitals, care centers and homeless shelters. They began with the three homeless shelters in the area: A Catholic one, one run by Presbyterians, and the other was non-denominational. Since the Catholic entity Saint Paul's Good Shepherd Center was the closest, it was their first stop. They arrived shortly before 7:30 as breakfast was being served to the guests. This was an ideal time to catch Father Joseph before he began his morning rituals.

After Hank introduced Robin and himself to the priest, the first thing he did was flash his NSA identity card. Father Joseph's reaction was, "Are you here in response to the call I made to the police yesterday afternoon?" When this was met by a quizzical look from the two visitors, the Father continued, "About the young man who came here yesterday. While he called himself "Sonny," I'm certain that wasn't his name. I got the feeling he was mixed up. Confused. Maybe didn't know his name. He didn't even know his age."

Robin leaned forward, eager to learn this might be Luke. "Can you describe him?"

"He was tall, thin and emaciated looking. His complexion was so white it looked like he had never been in the sun. When he took off his baseball cap, I could see his head had been shaved. Then I noticed a long scar on the side of his face, from here to here." Using his finger, the priest traced a line on his own face from his temple to the jaw. "I'd swear he just had some stitches removed.

The clothes didn't fit; looked like they were stolen from a hospital. My gut told me the guy needed help. His eyes bounced around, real nervous-like. I convinced him to spend the night with us and when he went to the back to get a bed, I called the cops. Then I got busy and forgot all about him. Later when I asked Sister Mary Alice to check on him, I found he must have snuck out. My guess is he went looking for the two men he became friends with when he was here."

Robin and Hank were certain this was their man. The G-man added, "Now we have to find him before Diego and Cam do. Those two must have joined forces to get Luke in order to demo the SoulTaker for the potential buyers.

CHAPTER THIRTY-TWO

The Same Day

If there was one thing CM3 was good at, it was intelligence. The company's expertise became unparalleled several years earlier after hiring Dutch Schultz to head up their security operation. If there was one area in which Sterling Claymore III excelled, it was surrounding himself with the best talent money could buy. In the field of corporate espionage, Dutch was in a class by himself. He had some traits in common with Claymore: exceedingly smart, deceitful, cunning, and the drive to stay one step ahead of his competition. It made no difference if what was required was unethical or illegal.

With the goal of capturing Luke and the SoulTaker, Dutch had managed to tap into NSA's communications. The first thing he did was to learn the latest on what the NSA knew about the search for Luke. Dutch was apprised of Hank Mitchell's various conversations with Luke's brother JD. In doing so he discovered Rafa's plans to sell the SLT system to unsavory foreigners who could use it for unethical purposes. It also led to learning Diego's new secret cell phone number which allowed him to continually monitor Diego's status in their search for Luke. Dutch was aware that Diego and Cam had joined forces, had possession of the SLT equipment, and had proceeded in their search for Luke. As of this time, Dutch knew Luke had escaped from the health center, and that Diego and Cam were combing the San Francisco area to find him. He also learned Rafa's group, Los Lomas, was under incredible pressure to complete a successful demo in order to make one hundred million dollars. The window of opportunity to stop the sale was fast approaching since the foreign scientists who were to attend the demonstration had travel visas which would expire in three more days. NSA was monitoring every move they were making. But Dutch wondered if the government agents assigned to validate their credentials and track their movement could have been bought off.

The head of security was also aware that Rafa's phone contacts with others regarding this mission were now being limited, including those with Diego. It made sense for the uncle to play everything close to the vest; he was too close to the huge payoff to have any kind of screwup. The exact time and place of the demonstration would probably come as early as Friday at a site in a San Francisco warehouse district. Dutch was preparing his team for various options. One part of his team would continue the search for Luke and the other would hunt down Diego and Cam.

CHAPTER THIRTY-THREE

February 26

In their quest to find Luke, Diego and Cam had been scouring parts of the city most accessible from the Los Pueblos Health Center where Luke had been held. Their search for more than six hours yesterday had been unsuccessful. So last night when they checked into the seedy motel Rafa had arranged, their failure was reflected in their listless, hunched-over postures.

At the hotel, Cam was given a separate room because it enabled him to retain control of the one thing he brought to the partnership—the SoulTaker equipment. Diego figured, as long as his partner possessed the SLT, he could rest easy knowing he would not be cut out of sharing in the one hundred-million-dollar payoff. Actually, Cam preferred his own approach better since he kept the vital microchip needed to operate the system in his money belt.

The motel was strategically located in the vicinity of the warehouse where Luke's demonstration was planned to take place. El Jefe, Rafa's boss at the cartel called him to say they were still waiting for confirmation on the date when the foreign scientists were available to observe the demo. They were optimistic it could take place within a week. On another matter, Rafa gave directions to the demo site location. To maintain confidentiality in case the call was being overheard, he did so in a clever way. "You'll set up the demo in the building across the street from where your old girlfriend used to live."

All three of them were aware this was crunch-time for finding Luke. Without him, there could be no demo. Diego remained optimistic about catching him because he was very likely in the immediate area. Then, once captured he would be tricked to divulge the algorithm so Diego could conduct the demonstration. At the close of their conversation, Rafa reminded the other two, "The stakes could not be higher. If we're not successful, our lives could be at risk."

* * *

Late morning, the next day, after Diego and Cam had been combing the area for several hours, Diego suddenly slammed on the brakes of their Toyota. It screeched to a halt narrowly missing two migrants sprawled on a park bench. Ahead they spotted a commotion of onlookers overflowing onto the street. It appeared the rowdy spectators had gathered near a Dutch Brothers coffee shop. A middle-aged man with a weathered face and sagging green eyes enthusiastically waved two greenbacks over his head screeching, "Free drinks. First come, first served." Fat Albert was flashing the cash he had filched from his new friend the previous night. Because of his height, that tall victim was easy to spot from a distance. Wearing an oversized Giants baseball cap, the man seemed befuddled by what was happening.

"My God, there's our guy! That's Luke," Diego shouted.

"Hang on, Diego," Cam yelled, bolting from the car. "I'll get him."

A few minutes earlier, while in search for something to eat, Luke's attention had been drawn to a familiar distinctive blue building. Spotting the Dutch Brothers coffee shop had enlivened some insatiable craving. Instantly, out of the blue, his favorite energy drink came to mind. *That's the treat I got every morning. My helper brought it to me while I studied test results. I can't remember her name.* At the moment he couldn't recall. But he did know she was important in his life. This comforting memory was abruptly interrupted by the forceful yank on his shoulder. A gruff voice came from someone he didn't know. "Luke! Luke! We've gotta get out of here." The sudden rudeness made Luke feel like he was under attack. Instinctively he lashed out. Cam deflected the punch and automatically countered with a blow to his gut that sent Luke crashing to the ground.

CHAPTER THIRTY-FOUR

The Same Day

After meeting with Father Joseph late yesterday afternoon, Robin and Hank had used the Good Shepherd homeless shelter as the epicenter of their systematic search for Luke. By evening, with their energy and confidence waning, they decided to call it a day. They checked into a nearby hotel.

It was midmorning the following day as they happened to be driving by a Dutch Brothers coffee shop, they noticed a strange commotion. A scuffle among spectators had overflowed onto the street. When Robin spied an iconic blue building, it generated familiar memories. Dutch Brothers was one of her regular haunts. It reminded her that the first thing she did every work day was to buy Luke his special drink. Noticing the unusual activity, she had a fleeting glance of a man who stood taller than the rest of the crowd. His string-bean stature seemed familiar. He looked ridiculous in his oversized baseball cap. Yesterday Father Joseph had described a visitor wearing a hat like that. Robin was stunned. Were her eyes playing tricks on her? Maybe she had Luke so much on her mind that it dominated all her thoughts. Was that really him? The more she thought about it, the more certain she was this was him.

"Hank," she gasped, "it's Luke. I just saw him. Stop the car and let me out."

Robin leaped from the vehicle before it came to a complete stop. The excitement of the moment gave her the strength of an amazon as she fought her way through the three-deep crowd. She was like a late-arriving spectator wrestling through the throng to find her seat at a championship fight. The onlookers she burrowed through marveled at the ferocity of being shoved aside by someone so ladylike.

Abruptly she popped through an opening in the ring of observers like a newborn bird breaking free from its shell. What she saw was a brawl that wasn't much of a contest. A husky aggressor was thrashing the hell out of a defenseless skinny guy huddling to protect himself. *That has to be Luke*, she thought. *God he's getting the hell beat out of him. Nobody's going to hurt you Baby. I'm here to save you.* Her adrenalin exploded off the Richter Scale. Recklessly, she launched her body at the bully with a fury, with no thought for her own safety. The bad guy's mouth flew open in fright by the onslaught of an unexpected attack. After ferociously propelling the aggressor to the ground, Robin's long fingernails scratched gashes in his face. His mug looked like it had been run through a meat grinder. Then she jerked hunks of hair from his scalp and sunk her teeth into his arm until it bled.

As she pulled the bully away, her attention turned to the defenseless guy sprawled face down on the grass in a fetal position. Something flashed across her mind. He had a birthmark on the back of his neck. Instantly this confirmed it was her work-partner. *My God, Luke. It is you! You look terrible. I'm here to help.*

The crowd had gone wild watching the frenzied female beat the crap out of the monster. When she turned to comfort the defenseless man, the crowd went ballistic.

Lying on the ground, a shocked Luke rolled over and gawked at his good-looking savior. As he touched her, their eyes met. He knew her but couldn't recall why. Then suddenly, he cried, "You saved me!"

Before she could react, Cam pounced on her unmercifully like a crazed warrior. He smashed his right elbow into the side of her face. She dropped to the ground like a hundred-pound sack of flour. She was out cold. A three-inch slash along her jaw began to bleed profusely. Fortunately, being unconscious saved her from agonizing pain. Not only had his blow broken four of her ribs, but the elbow to her face created a gash that would require dozens of stitches.

As Luke studied the attacker, he had no clue as to who or where he was. Even without the memory loss, he would have no idea why this stranger had assaulted both of them. It would have been beyond his wildest dreams to know that the SLT he invented was worth millions of dollars and that enemies in foreign countries planned to use it to inflict so much damage. Furthermore, there was no way he could he have imagined his former neurology partner Diego was working with a Las Vegas detective and a Mexican cartel to make this happen.

Then Hank burst onto the scene. After slamming the assailant to the ground, he recognized it was one of the men he had been chasing. *This is payback time.* With that, he gave the tyrant a well-deserved kick in the crotch causing the attacker to groan as he withered to the ground. The resulting whimper was music to Hank's ears. He gave a gratified smile as he flashed his NSA badge to the cheering onlookers.

After the crowd dissolved, Hank began to understand what had energized his mild-mannered companion. He hurried to Robin's side to give her his undivided attention. After a few minutes she revived, thanks to help from a doctor who had been observing the fracas.

Hank had been so concerned about her recovery his complete focus was on being there for her. A couple of minutes later, she muttered, "Lu-Lu-Luke." Anxiously, the agent's eyes darted around to see what had happened to the skinny guy who had been beaten to a pulp. That surely had to be Luke and Robin would have identified him regardless of how battered he looked. But Luke was gone. In a flash, everything fell into place. While his attention had slipped from keeping an eye on Cam, he vaguely remembered some bystander coming to Luke's aid. Could that have been Diego?

At least Hank had Cameron Dalton. He beamed with satisfaction at having caught one of the villains. His interrogation should lead to finding Luke as well as Diego. So, he turned to see how Cam was recovering from his well-placed boot. Then his mouth dropped. *Where is he? How could he have gotten away?* Never in his life had he let a crook escape. Maybe it was time to think seriously about retiring.

CHAPTER THIRTY-FIVE
The Same Day

Seeing a savior come to his rescue was a welcome sight for Luke. But no one seemed to know or care as he was being guided away from the scene. With a comforting arm around his shoulder, Luke felt secure that his colleague had come to his rescue.

A sudden spark of memory enabled him to recognize his friend, but not his name. *He's my friend, right? But why do I have mixed feelings about him? I worked with him. He helped on my invention. He was great. But why did he leave me? I'm confused.*

Suddenly, the cloud started to lift. *I know who he is. He's Diego, Diego Reyes.* "It's Diego, right? Isn't that your name?" Luke asked, trying to show some confidence in his memory.

"Sure, Luke. I can't tell you how good it is to have found you."

Then, with a fogginess in his eyes, Luke added, "Didn't we have some sort of falling out? Guess it must not have been too bad. You seem to be happy to see me."

"I sure am. You disappeared after having some sort of accident. It's great to see you. I've missed our working together."

"Yeah," Luke muttered. "Guess I'm still confused. I thought we had a misunderstanding and you left."

"Naw, you know how I am. Sometimes, when I have problems, I get moody." Diego forced a winning smile and patted his partner on the shoulder. Then with a caring grip on Luke's arm, he added,

"I'm here to help you." He pointed to a car not far away and added, "We're going home."

"Home, that sounds good. Where are we anyway? What am I doing here?"

"One question at a time, Buddy. You wandered away and got into some sort of accident. Everything's going to be all right. You just need some rest. Then, you'll feel better in no time.

"We've been looking for you for several days. Right now, we're in San Francisco. But we're sure glad we found you. I've got to get you ready for your big presentation. In the meantime, I've got you a place to stay."

"Huh?"

"In a couple of days, you're going to show some very important people what your new invention the SoulTaker can do."

About thirty minutes later the two friends had checked into a motel where they would share a room. Luke stretched himself out on one of the beds. He wasn't as confident about his recall as he hoped. *The cloud is beginning to lift. But what I'm remembering is coming in pieces.* Suddenly both hands shot to his temples as he emitted a frantic groan. "Gosh, I've got one heck of a headache. Feels like I've been in a prizefight."

"Well, you were. Some big guy attacked you. Must have been for your money," Diego lied.

"What were we talking about?"

"About working together. At JIT's neurology lab."

"Oh yeah, . . . at Jobs." There was a twinkle in Luke's eye. "It's starting to come back to me now."

Diego took the opportunity to cash in on his supposed friendship. "Luke, you've been setting the world on fire with your inventions. First you built a way for people to monitor their own health. And then you've been developing a system to communicate telepathically with others. You use a laser to find out what they're thinking. Remember?"

"It's a little hazy. I think I was excited by its possibilities." The change in his facial expression showed he was struggling with recall. Then, a light went on. "I sort of remember. But I was bothered. Wasn't I bothered about using it to invade a person's privacy. That wouldn't be good to have that much power over others. I think it troubled me so much, I didn't want to pursue it."

"You were right," Diego lied. "I was skeptical, too. But you became convinced the benefits of using it outweighed its difficulties. And you persuaded me it was okay, that is, under strictly controlled circumstances."

The concern on Luke's face suggested he was troubled by what Diego had said.

Realizing this, Diego quickly changed the subject. He needed to reassure Luke they still had a good relationship. Sympathetically, he said, "You were right, Luke, when you felt I left the lab because I was unhappy. I was, but it had nothing to do with you. I was under a lot of stress. I don't know if you remember me telling you, my uncle suffered terribly from pancreatic cancer. He was the dad I never had. I was his only relative. His health problems were more than he could handle alone. And it turned out my helping him was more than I could take. It affected my relationships with others. I just wasn't myself. It made me lash out. I was difficult to be around. I apologize for not treating you like the good friend you were. Or are, I should say. I wasn't making good decisions. Uncle Rafa demanded I take care of him; hold his hand or whatever he needed to get him through his pain. So, I took this out on you. I left in a hurry without even saying goodbye."

"Gee, I'm so sorry. How's he doing now?"

"He died. What a horrible way to go. The other day, when I called to apologize for the way I acted, I learned you were gone. Robin suggested I call your brother because the two of you are close."

"Oh yeah, JD," Luke replied hesitantly, like he was still searching to fill in the blanks of his memory. "Diego, you're going to have to help me. I'm having one heck of a time remembering things. Guess I was in some sort of accident and put in a place that wasn't very friendly. I thought the meds I was taking were overdosing me. I felt more like a prisoner than a patient. So, when I got the chance, I escaped. Now that my memory is starting to return, I just want to go home to rest and sort things out. Can you help me?"

"That's exactly what I'm going to do," Diego said.

CHAPTER THIRTY-SIX

The Same Day

A few minutes later, Luke rested on the motel bed feeling he was recovering from being blacked out. While still exhausted, he struggled to clear up some confusion. *Why am I here? What the heck's going on? I know my memory is not the best. But he said he's going to take me home.*

His anxiety increased to the point where he couldn't lay still. *Can I really trust him? He needs my help. What's my gut telling me?* Screwing up his face, Luke strained to ponder what had been happening. *Take it easy*, he chastised himself. *I can't expect to remember everything at once. I have to rely on those who are concerned about me. Like that woman who saved me from my beating. The look in her eyes said she cared about me. We must have been close. What was her name? Ra . . Ra . . Robin, yes Robin. What a tiger. She was ferocious. She must care for me a lot. Why else would she have taken on that brute?* A smile formed on his lips. *She beat the crap out of him.*

The world was opening up before his very eyes. *I'll get through this. Thank God I've got friends who are looking out for me. I just need to trust them. They'll pull me through this.*

Abruptly he scowled from the searing pain radiating through his head. Instantly one hand shot to his forehead. The sensation was exactly like what he once experienced when gulping down a large scoop of ice cream. The discomfort was excruciating. For a moment he was totally debilitated.

"Are you all right?" Diego asked as he moved near Luke, grasping his arm to console him.

After a moment, Luke replied, "Yeah, I'll be fine. It just happened so fast."

Diego replied, "You're reacting to the concussion. The doctor said you were fortunate to have come through this as well as you have."

"What caused it?"

"Evidently you were fighting to defend the honor of a woman at a bar in San Francisco. You got clobbered by some drunk. Ended up in the hospital, then intensive care."

Me, defend a woman? At a bar? Gosh, I don't go to bars. I hardly ever drink.

"How long ago was that?" Luke asked.

"Almost two weeks ago."

"What day is it now?"

"It's Wednesday, February 26."

The look on Luke's face showed confusion.

This conversation was not going the way Diego hoped. He had wanted the neurologist to feel comfortable and trusting. Luke was vulnerable and this was the perfect opportunity for Diego to squeeze out of him the algorithm needed to operate the SLT.

Diego gave another fib hoping to achieve his goal. "We can get into what happened to you a little later. Right now, I need your help on an urgent matter. It has to do with your SoulTaker device. Representatives of the INS are now meeting in San Francisco."

"INS?"

"The International Neurological Society."

"Oh yeah."

"They're putting together a list of candidates for this year's Outstanding Achievement Awards. It's a prestigious honor and Dr. Abbott submitted the SoulTaker as an entry. He believes winning this honor would be great PR for JIT."

Luke gave a nod to this suggestion, but otherwise didn't seem overly excited.

Diego continued, "Anyway, you'd be doing your boss a favor by demonstrating what your machine can do. You'd be willing to do that, wouldn't you?"

"Yeah, I suppose so. Anything for the school and Phil." Luke suddenly realized that referring to Dr. Abbott as "Phil" meant his memory was improving.

Since being taken hostage, Luke was not aware that his device had been stolen. And Diego was not about to mention that it was now under Cam's control and was hidden in the very room next door.

"Would you be willing to demonstrate the device for the INS committee?"

"I suppose so."

"Do you remember the code you need to open it up to operate?" Although Diego's hands were sweating, he tried to act as calm as possible.

At this moment for Diego, knowing this code was more important than anything else in the world. Because with that key, he could operate the SoulTaker as he had done several times before under Luke's close supervision.

As Luke's memory began to improve, he vaguely remembered why Diego might have been so upset. Was it because he would not share that operating code? Luke was not about to share the code with anyone until he figured out a way to protect others from unwittingly exposing confidential information. In working with Diego over several months, Luke seemed to remember questioning his morals and trustworthiness. This led Luke to develop a code that could be changed daily. The solution was a formula using the specific day of the month, thus causing the code to change each day.

So, when Diego asked for the code, Luke spilled out the answer. "9905."

Diego breathed a sigh of relief as Luke matter-of-factly spewed out the number. Luke's never sharing that secret formula before was why Diego had left the lab several months ago. Originally expecting no cooperation from Luke, he and his uncle figured they would have to coerce Luke to perform the demonstration for the buyers. But what now happened was even better. Having this code meant he could unlock the device and operate it on his own. Little did he know this encryption was only good for the day.

Being a mathematical genius, Luke had made the computation in his head. He prided himself in calculating numbers in his head faster than most using a calculator. His code to unlock the SLT was figuring out the first four significant digits in the square root of the day of the month, and then reversing the order. He mentally computed the square root of today's date, the twenty-sixth, which was 5.099 and then reversed the sequence to give him 9905. For today no other combination of numbers could open the device. The neurologist felt good about doing this, because it confirmed his thinking was improving.

Diego was overjoyed at learning the answer. Hurriedly he jotted "9905" on a scrap of paper and stuffed it into his wallet for safekeeping. What he was not aware of was that this series of numbers was only good for today.

As Diego pocketed his note, there was a light rap on the door. He cautiously opened the door only a crack to see it was Cam. The bedraggled detective looked as though he had been run over by a Pershing tank. Diego wondered if his pitiful appearance was partially due to the humiliation of being thoroughly beaten by a woman. Tactfully, he decided to not mention that. Quickly, Diego raised his hand to hush his partner from saying anything. When he peeked over his shoulder, he noticed an exhausted Luke straining to see who was at the door. Returning his attention to Cam, he nodded in the direction of his room next door as he mouthed, "I've got him, and better yet, I have the code. Go clean yourself up and I'll be right over." To Luke, he said, "It's nothing important. Just the maid wondering if I needed anything." Once he closed the door, Diego went to the bathroom, extracted a bottle of Avinol PM sleeping tablets from Luke's daub kit, meted out a double dose, and took them along with a glass of water to his prisoner. He said, "Here take these. It'll help you sleep. You'll feel much better when you wake up."

The weariness on Luke's pale face was accompanied by a steely stare. He uttered, "You know, Diego, there's only one thing that'll make me feel better."

"What's that?"

"Getting me the hell out of here. I want to go home. And I mean right now."

"We'll do that soon. First, I have one thing to take care of. It won't take long. But I can't leave until you take those pills. So, the sooner you do, the sooner I can go do my errand."

In a sign of impatience, Luke folded his arms across his chest and blurted, "You can go to hell." This was accompanied by a grimace suggesting that for the first time Diego might not have his best interest at heart. *Does this have something to do with the SoulTaker? Does he want to unlock it and run it on his own. At least my one salvation is the code I gave him will only work for the rest of today.* "Damn Diego, I'm not going to take any pills!"

"Have it your way, my friend," Diego said, as he marched to the bathroom. A couple of minutes later when he returned, Luke could see his supposed friend was carrying a syringe and a vial. It was obvious to see what his caretaker had in mind. "You've given me no choice, Luke. You're too exhausted to go anywhere. This will help you rest while I do my chore, and then we'll be on our way."

Using all of his resistance to fend off the injection wasn't enough. With an overpowering grip on his arm, Diego easily administered the dose.

You're going to do something with the SoulTaker, aren't you? What a fool I've been for giving you that code. Whatever you do, you'd better do it today. Luke gave a wry smile barely able to finish this thought as his reasoning wilted faster than a pat of butter in a scorching sun.

By this time Diego was leaving. Locking the door behind him, he slipped next door.

A short time later, while waiting for Cam to finish cleaning up, Diego phoned his uncle to report what had been happening. "Hey Rafa, I know I'm not supposed to contact you. But you'll be glad I did. I've got fantastic news. Not only do I have Luke, I also have the code to open the SLT."

After a pause, his uncle replied, "That's good to know. But Jee-sus Chrie-est, can't you ever follow directions. You're supposed to keep our contact to the absolute minimum. Right now, the Feds could be listening in and, if so, they'll know what you've done. All you had to do was text me with the codes we set up. Remember: '1, 2, 3' which meant: 1, I've got Luke, 2, he's cooperating with us, and 3, he gave me the code. How could it be simpler than that? Now go do '4.' That means run a test on the SoulTaker to show the damn thing works. Listen carefully. Here's what you'll –"

Diego interrupted, "Sorry about that. Just figured you'd be pleased as hell."

"Well, I am. But now we've got to know it works."

"Okay, so we'll head to the site where you set things up and I'll run the test."

Rafa said, "I've arranged everything exactly as you told me. It will be easy for you to connect all of the parts according to your instructions." Then, the uncle added, "I've got some good news for you, too. The buyers are ready to see the demo sooner than we originally planned. They're as eager as we are to get this done and leave the country. They can do this as early as tomorrow afternoon. Say, two in the afternoon. I'll assume that's good for you once you send me the signal that everything works. When can I expect that?"

"Uncle, this isn't as simple as connecting a couple of parts and turning on the switch. First, I've got to train Cam to be the subject I'm testing. That will take some time for everything to be coordinated. Then I've got to make sure I know how to evaluate the information I get from the interview. This whole thing will probably take at least four or five hours." Checking his watch Diego added, "I should have everything done by nine tonight. . . or ten at the latest."

"All right, nephew. Just signal me with a text using the number '4.' That's it. Don't screw it up. Then by tomorrow night, we can celebrate. I'll buy you a margarita. Hell, I'll buy you an entire tequila factory. . . Hasta luego."

As soon as Diego ended the call, he and Cam took off for the testing site. Cam took along the SoulTaker device, supporting equipment and operating manual. Diego brought his file of notes accumulated during the time spent with Luke in developing the device and, especially important was the four-digit code Luke had given him to unlock the system.

CHAPTER THIRTY-SEVEN

The Same Day

CM3's head of security had a reputation for being a step ahead of his competition when it came to gathering timely developments on his assignments. This remained true when a member of his team gave him the detailed particulars of Diego's conversation with his uncle. That took place only a few minutes ago. It also included the location from where Diego's call had been made. As the search for Luke was ramping up, Dutch could feel the adrenalin flowing through his veins. He loved the chase, especially when it concerned such an important undertaking for his boss. This was one of his most exciting missions in thirty-three years of sleuthing. Lust was in his blood. He'd gladly do this job without pay except he enjoyed the perks too much. He had a home in San Diego's exclusive Torrey Hills district with a Jaguar parked in a three-stall garage, membership at the Coronado Country Club and the freedom to do whatever he wanted when not on duty. Dutch was amused that his social contacts never knew about the sleazy operations he conducted each day.

This morning Dutch had heard from one of his associates that Luke had been sighted at a Dutch Brothers coffee shop on the lower east side of San Francisco. The head of security considered it ironic that this mission involved a facility bearing his first name. This had to be an omen of forthcoming success. One of his staff had been cruising that area in search of Luke when his attention was drawn to a fracas. Dutch was notified immediately. As the activity wound down, his CM3 man caught a glimpse of NSA agent Hank Mitchell tending to a battered female. Since he was well aware that

Robin Hunt had joined them in the search for Luke, it seemed likely she could have been the injured woman. Also, it was noted that Luke's attacker was Cameron Dalton, who had escaped capture by Mitchell.

From this report and learning of Diego's conversation with his uncle, Dutch was able to fill in the blanks. After Luke had been attacked by Cameron Dalton, he left the scene with Diego's help. He was escorted to a motel where Diego and Cam already possessed the SoulTaker. And since Diego had worked with Luke in designing the invention, he then was in a position to obtain the code to operate the device. This meant the bad guys were ready to demonstrate the SoulTaker for foreign buyers.

At this point, Dutch figured the Feds would also likely be privy to this information. In order to beat NSA to saving Luke and stopping the sale of the device, he needed to take bold action right away. But because this mission was so important to Claymore, Dutch felt obligated to get the CEO's blessing of what he had in mind.

After hearing his security man's report, the CEO said, "I like what you've got in mind. If we do this right, we can befriend Luke and be the one to control the SoulTaker. We'll make a fortune." Then the boss added, "Somehow, I'm going to have to get Luke's trust to operate the damned thing. I'll let him know we're on his side and will support him in doing whatever he feels is best. That means getting him home, giving him time to recoup and let him be reunited with his girlfriend. If I'm lucky, I'll get him to work for us. We'll make him an offer he can't refuse. That'll include giving him an unlimited budget to continue his own research operation. That's what turns him on. The guy is so creative, he'll make a fortune for us."

By mid-afternoon, Dutch had assembled an assault team and was at the office of the seedy motel where Diego had rented two rooms. Outfitted with police uniforms, the manager immediately led them to the targeted rooms.

In Diego's room, Dutch discovered Luke unconscious. Although he looked as though he had gone several rounds with an over-matched prizefighter, he was sleeping soundly. A physician accompanying the team diagnosed he had been drugged. But it was not from the pills resting on the nightstand next to his bed. The bruising on his left upper arm and a needle mark suggested he had been injected with some substance to knock him out. Despite obvious superficial injuries, his vital signs remained strong.

While there was no sign of Diego and Cam, Dutch was confident they were in the vicinity. More than likely, they were in a building somewhere in the warehouse district preparing for tomorrow's demonstration of the SoulTaker for foreign buyers.

Immediately upon being informed of Luke's rescue, the CM3 boss ordered Dutch to deliver the neurologist to the Zuckerberg San Francisco General Hospital for a thorough medical examination. Claymore knew that hospital's administrator and was confident he could have immediate access to Luke's status.

CHAPTER THIRTY-EIGHT
The Same Day

As Luke was being transferred to the Zuckerberg hospital, Hank waited anxiously in another medical facility to support Robin. Rather than turning this responsibility over to one of his underlings, he stayed with her to ensure she received the best care available.

Thanks to a close friend who was an orthopedic surgeon at the UCSF Medical Center in San Francisco, Hank arranged for her to get swift attention at a medical facility on the Parnassus Heights campus.

During his wait in the lobby, Hank studied updates on what the NSA and other Fed operations knew about the SoulTaker investigation. He learned of El Jefe's conversation with the Mexican boss of Mazatlán's Los Lomas drug cartel. The demo had been scheduled to take place at 2 p.m. tomorrow. The price on the sale of the SoulTaker system to a foreign consortium had been finalized. One hundred million US dollars was now available in INK's Swiss bank account. INK was the Iranian-North Korean joint venture created to purchase the SLT system. The Colombian drug dealer who put the transaction together had negotiated the distribution of funds with Rafa's boss. Half of the money was to be paid upon delivery of the SoulTaker, and the balance would be distributed thirty days later upon satisfactory performance of the device. Los Lomas was not happy with the temporary hold placed on part of the funds. However, while they were used to being paid up front, the extraordinary size of this transaction made the wait worthwhile. The initial fifty million dollars would to be split accordingly: $5 million to the Colombian contractor who found the buyer and negotiated the deal, $22.5 million to Los Lomas, and $22.5 million to Rafa, from which Diego and Cam would each receive $5 million. Thirty days later the second round of similar payments would take place. Although Diego had initially come up with this idea, his share was far more money than he could have ever conceived of earning in his lifetime.

While waiting for word on the results of Robin's examination, Hank continued following up on loose ends in the investigation. He directed his associates to search for the site where Diego would conduct Sunday's demo. He felt a lead might come from the files the Feds already had on Los Lomas cocaine operations in San Francisco, including locations Rafa might have used for distributing drugs. The agent also suggested trying to track down the scientists who represented the buyers from North Korea and Iran since they were attending a neurology conference in town.

Then he contacted JD and Dr. Abbott and brought them up to speed. He asked if they had any other suggestions worth pursuing.

Two hours later, while remaining in the lobby, Hank received a face-time cell call from his surgeon friend who had made the arrangement for Robin's care. "I've got a report from the doctor ministering to Robin. She's gone through a hell of a beating. But the news is positive. She's been diagnosed with four broken ribs. One of them is in danger of penetrating her lungs. But that can be taken care of in short order. The only other concern is the two-inch gash on her jaw."

Hank knew this had been caused by Cam's flailing elbow during their brawl.

The surgeon continued, "I've got a terrific plastic surgeon on my staff who can perform a miracle on her face. He'll be over to see her in the next couple of hours. Hank, you can rest assured, when he's done, she'll keep her pristine appearance."

"Mack, you're terrific. I want to thank you for personally following through on this. I owe you big time."

"It's my pleasure. You don't owe me a thing. I can never thank you enough for what you did for my kid."

The smile of satisfaction on Hank's face showed that comment warmed his heart. He recalled that about twenty years ago, he had guided Mack's youngster through the arduous recovery of his battle with hard drugs.

Before leaving the hospital, the agent stopped by the gift shop where he picked up the most expensive bouquet of flowers and a note card. When he entered Robin's room, she was sleeping peacefully. He gave her a thoughtful peck on the forehead, then dropped the note on the tray within easy reach of her. The message on the note read, "If you didn't have such a promising future at the lab, I'd hire you in a minute. I admire your tenacity in our search for Luke."

CHAPTER THIRTY-NINE

The Same Day

It had been only about an hour since Luke had divulged the algorithm needed to operate the SoulTaker. Now the two men who had captured him were eager to make sure the code worked and that the device functioned properly.

About fifteen minutes after receiving it, Diego and Cam were at the site Rafa had selected for the demo. The building was located in a part of the warehouse district only a few blocks from his uncle's office. It was a desolate area where no one was around to notice anything going on.

A combination lock on the front door made for easy access. Upon entering and flipping on the lights, they noticed a musty odor, but the concrete floor was immaculate suggesting a caretaker had been hard at work. The barren interior held shipping cartons along the walls. Ceiling lights hanging from the rafters gave the dramatic appearance of a stage where something important could take place.

In the center of the room were two four-by-six-foot tables covered with neatly arranged paraphernalia. The tables were surrounded by a dozen folding chairs. This arrangement reminded Cam of pioneers preparing for an Indian attack with the circling of their wagons. The myriad of electrical cords extending from the work area looked like octopus tentacles. Everything seemed neatly arranged and ready for a hookup with the SLT.

"What an impressive setting," Cam said.

"Yeah, just like the doctor ordered," Diego replied. "Now let's see if he's got everything here that I asked for."

Cam reverently took the SoulTaker and its supporting equipment from his attaché case and placed them on the table. The care in which he did so suggested this was the most important possession of his life.

After reviewing the information in the operating manual and his work-notes, Diego was anxious to see if he could operate the device. Minutes later the connections were ready to be tested.

Diego had never been more exhilarated. "The Gods are with us," he boasted. "Spotting Luke in the crowd at that coffee shop was meant to be."

Cam snarled, "You're right, but not about me being mauled by that crazy woman."

Diego said, "Well, the beating you took made capturing Luke possible. It kept everyone's attention on you while I led him away. And my meeting him could not have gone better. His memory was so bad he didn't remember how bad I wanted him to share the code with me. Well, I managed to convince him we were still good friends. So, I fed him a story about his invention being considered for some prestigious scientific award. When he heard this, he became cooperative. Just like that, he spilled the beans giving me the code to unlock the device. I've written it here on this piece of paper." He yanked it from his pocket, flagging it in the air. "Buddy, we are home free. All we have to do now is run a test to make sure it works.

When Diego clicked the activation switch on the laser gun nothing happened. He tried again. Still no luck.

"Jesus," he bellowed in frustration, "what the fuck's going on? This has never happened before." Using more force, he pounded the switch with the heel of his hand. Once again, nothing happened. Drops of perspiration began to form on his forehead. Another slap at the switch produced the same result.

Shaking his head in exasperation, Diego said, "Fuck it, Cam, I don't know what's wrong."

As Diego fiddled with the gun, Cam probed his waist and fished out a tiny piece of shiny metal from his money belt. Presenting it to his partner, he slyly asked, "Is this what you're looking for?"

"What are you talking about? What's that?"

"The operators' manual says this is the microchip needed to operate the system. It also houses the code mechanism which remembers the combination to unlock the device."

"Damn you Cam," Diego said, wiping the sweat from his forehead. "Why in the hell did you take that out?"

"To protect my interest. I didn't want to be cut out of the deal. I knew you couldn't run it without this chip. So as long as I kept it, you needed me. Now that we're close to the payoff, I figured my share is safe."

"What a shitty trick to pull."

"Come on, Diego, you'd have done the same if you were in my shoes."

The look on his face confirmed that was true.

Cam then popped the chip into where it belonged. He had been pretty sure Diego had never learned how to do this because Luke only let Diego operate the device after he had entered his secret code.

A short time later the SLT was ready to run. Turning to his partner, Diego said, "Say a prayer. It's all or nothing."

With a deep breath, he glanced at the piece of paper showing the four-digit code Luke had given him and entered "9905" into the keyboard. Suddenly luminous green symbols lit up the digital reader making it look like a slot machine at a casino. For what seemed like forever, but was actually less than thirty seconds, random numbers flashed on the screen until 9905 was recognized. Quickly the monitor came to life. "By God, we're in! This baby's going to work. . . Now Cam, it's time to review what your role's going to be. You're going to be the one to communicate with the SoulTaker to test out the system."

"This won't be dangerous, right?" Cam asked.

"No problem, Luke and I've done this a lot. I'll take good care of you." He was careful not to mention the hazards involved. When Diego last assisted in testing the program on humans, their experiments revealed about three percent of the volunteers experienced various types of brain trauma. A few even ended up in a clinic where studies revealed some neurological damage; one developed a chronic migraine with no relief in sight. Diego felt Luke had probably resolved those issues by now. At this time the detective's welfare was of no concern to him, as long as the visiting scientists observed no problem.

The information extracted during Cam's testing proved the device functioned well. It gathered information on a wide range of subjects. However, the exhaustive testing took far more time than expected. After more than five hours of cautious trial and error, Diego proved he could not only collect Cam's innermost thoughts, but influence some of his attitudes. Luke's former assistant seemed blown away by the sophisticated improvements added since he last tested the model at the lab.

As he was completing the final phase of testing, Diego's cell buzzed. The call was from his uncle who sounded exasperated.

"Why in the hell haven't you called to say that the damned thing's working? I expected to hear something several hours ago."

"Uncle, I haven't been sitting around. This system is complex. A lot more so than when I worked on it several months ago. It's working great now. You're going to be very pleased. I was just finishing one final check and was about ready to send you the signal."

"That's a relief. I was afraid we'd have a terrible problem if you failed."

"Why? What do you mean?" Diego asked.

"Everything depends on you. Luke can't help us anymore. He's gone. The Feds tracked him down and took him away."

"Holy shit! How did you get word?"

"On the police scanner. They found him at the motel. Guess they weren't able to talk with him. He was plenty doped up. But it sounds like he'll survive."

"Thank God we got what we needed from him. You can now rest easy, Uncle. The SoulTaker is fully operational."

"Well, you're going to have to find another place to stay tonight. The Feds are swarming around looking for you. Just remember to be well prepared before the demo tomorrow. I've made arrangements for the scientists to join you at three o'clock. Not at two as we originally scheduled."

By the time the two men left the test site it was almost midnight. Despite losing Luke and knowing the Feds were hot on their tail, they were in a triumphant mood. They took with them the SLT device but left behind the gear Rafa's team had provided. That would make it easier to set up for tomorrow afternoon's demonstration.

As they left to look for another motel, a smile crept over Diego's face. *Soon I'm going to be a millionaire, five times over. And a month later there'll be another five million put in the Cayman Islands account Rafa set up for me.*

CHAPTER FORTY
February 27

It was after two in the morning when Diego and Cam finally found a safe place to stay because the cops had to be staking out the motel where Luke had been found. While the SLT demonstration had been set for mid-afternoon, by 6:15 in the morning Luke's former assistant was too excited to sleep any longer. The adrenalin coursing through Diego's veins made him as antsy as a bug dancing in a hot skillet. The heavy breathing coming from the other bed didn't help the situation. Several minutes of listening to the wheezing rebounding off the walls suggested his partner was content. *Cam, how can you just lay there when this is the most significant day of your life?* A glance at his watch revealed it was 6:40. *I know we've got almost seven hours until the demo, but I can't lollygag around here anymore. I won't be comfortable until everything's set up and tested one more time. This is too important to screw up.*

With that, Diego rolled out of bed and shook his partner's shoulder saying, "Hey, Cam, you've got to get up. Today is the big day. We've got to head back to the warehouse and make sure everything is ready for this afternoon."

"Err. . err. . what're you saying?" came the groggy reply. "What time is it anyway?"

"It's almost seven."

"What the hell is the big rush. Everything went well last night. This is going to be a piece of cake."

When Cam rolled over, Diego shook him harder.

The detective responded, "Yeah. . . Yeah, get me a Bloody Mary. That'll get me going."

After more coaxing and a cold shower, Cam got with the program. Then, over big breakfasts the men approached the day from different perspectives. Nervously, Diego spoke rapidly, focusing on every detail of the work ahead. Coming out of his grogginess, Cam lackadaisically dragged his toast through runny eggs intent on having a leisurely meal. Eventually, the younger of the two felt any more of his lectures on their roles in the demo would be of little use. So, he said, "Come on man, let's get going. We'll both feel better once we know everything's set for our show."

Even though two hours of testing would have seemed adequate to prepare for the demo, the pair arrived at the test site four hours early. With so much money riding on a successful demonstration, they were eager to ensure the SoulTaker would be in perfect working order.

With a queasy stomach, Diego tapped the code into the keyboard expecting to see the monitor flash acknowledging the entry of 9905 would open the system. But nothing happened. After a second failure, he spotted the crumpled paper that he had thrown on the floor last night, confirmed he was using the correct code, and tried one more. Still, the activation did not work.

Cam gave an uneasy glance at his partner. Sweat was dripping down Diego's face. It made him look like he just stepped out of a shower. It was accompanied by an intense frown.

The detective thought of Murphy's Law: *Anything that can go wrong will go wrong.* Turning to his partner, he asked, "What's the problem? You've been tinkering with that too long."

Diego wiped his brow with his forearm, then said, "We've got a problem. I can't get the damn thing to unlock." Pointing to the crumpled paper he said, "Those fucking numbers worked last night. I know they're right. But now they don't work."

"It's a good thing we came early," Cam said.

With a disgusted scowl, Diego replied, "Hell, coming here early doesn't mean a fucking thing. I just can't get the son of a bitch to work."

"Huh?"

After thinking about it for a moment, Diego's face turned red. He muttered, "That Luke is a conniving bastard. I know what he did."

"What's that?"

"The number he gave me was only good for yesterday. He's programmed it to change every day. Last night we tried the code several times to make sure it worked. Right? But this morning it doesn't. There has to be a different code for today. Without it, we're screwed. We've gotta find Luke and get the new one. Rafa's going to shit when he hears this."

"God, Diego, how're we going to do that. The cops have him. Even if we were lucky enough to track him down, we'd never be back here in time for the demo."

Gritting his teeth, Diego glumly said, "Our only choice is for Rafa to postpone the meeting. This is too important to give him this news over the phone. He's got to come over to show him it's not working."

*   *   *

Less than half an hour later, Diego's uncle arrived to learn of the problem. The shock froze him for a moment. After recovering, he said, "The first thing I've got to do is let El Jefe know. Our demo has to be delayed and hopefully he can help us come up with a way to find Luke. The Colombia group will have our hide if we fail on this sale. Torture and murder are only a couple of things we could face. Even our families are in danger."

Before calling the Los Lomas cartel, the three men hunkered down at the table to consider possible alternatives. Finally, Rafa concluded, "I've got to tell El Jefe that we have no choice but to delay the demo. I know the scientists want to leave the country as soon as possible, but now they'll have to stick around and fly out Sunday night. In the meantime, we somehow have to track down Luke and force him to help. This is really going to piss off Estevez." Juan Estevez was the drug lord of the Medellin cartel.

Grave concern showed on Rafa's face. He had never been involved in anything of this magnitude; especially one that could have such devastating consequences.

Nervousness showed in Rafa's call to El Jefe. After explaining the dire situation, he asked, "Does the Medellin have any contacts in the States who could help us track down Luke? Where he is now is anyone's guess."

"Bringing the Medellin in on this has gotta be the last thing we'd do. They've put a lot of dough in this project and if it fails, they'll lose face. Rafa, we need to handle this ourselves." Then he continued, "Got any ideas on might have happened to Luke?" El Jefe asked.

"The police scanner said he was rescued from the motel. At first we thought the cops took him. But our police contact believes he was taken by some group impersonating them. No mention was made of Luke's condition or where he was. The best leads on his whereabouts seem to be those close to him: his brother JD Pope, Dr. Abbott, and Robin Hunt. There's gotta be others, but right now we can't think of any."

"I can't tell you how much of a setback this is for us. Before I'd ever consider calling Colombia, I'd want to get more information through some of my contacts or boys. Give me a little time. I'll get back to you."

After ending the discussion with El Jefe and Rafa had left, Diego turned to Cam and said, "I don't see the need of continuing to cart that damn stuff around anymore." He motioned with a sweep of his hand to all the parts of the SoulTaker that Cam had taken from the Desert Vault which had been deposited there by Luke. "Let's box them up in the container Luke used and stash them in one of the cartons over by the front door.

"Sounds good to me," Cam replied.

A couple of minutes later the parts had been stored in Luke's three containers. They were hidden in the carton, second from the bottom on the far-left end. The carton number was XL 520613.

"I'll remember that number because I'm extra-large and my shoe size is 13," Cam said.

"Just in case we run into any problem, I'll call Rafa and give him that information."

After doing so, the two locked the front door and headed to the motel that had served them well the previous night.

CHAPTER FORTY-ONE

February 27

Almost eighteen hours earlier Luke had been rescued by Dutch Schultz and his detail of "impersonating officers." Friday, yesterday morning, Luke began receiving a thorough physical and mental examination at the Zuckerberg hospital in San Francisco.

This morning, all reports appeared to be as good as could be expected under the circumstances. Despite not believing in even modest exercise, the inventor's health had remained excellent thanks to good genes and a fairly satisfactory diet. Although physically feeling like a limp dishrag, his attitude was improving. With his memory showing remarkable improvement he had been able to recall who he was, where he worked, and thoughts about his workmate Robin.

The hospital administrator had been calling Sterling Claymore in San Diego with progress reports several times a day since Luke had been admitted. Around seven o'clock this morning, CM3's CEO was permitted to speak with the patient on a face-time connection.

"Good morning, Dr. Pope, this is Sterling Claymore. I've been following your progress with great interest. I understand you have been making an extraordinary recovery. You look pretty healthy and, as I understand it, you may be released soon. We haven't had an opportunity to officially meet, but I'm looking forward to doing so in the very near future."

"Thank you for calling. I know a good deal about you. Phil has told me about the generous proposals you've been making to JIT. He sees a great partnership in our working together," Luke said.

"You've certainly got that right, Son."

Luke replied with a wince in his face showing he didn't appreciate the man's idea of trying to exert control over his invention.

Claymore continued, "While you were sleeping last night, your nurse said you mumbled 'Robin.'"

Yeah, I'm sure I did. Luke thought. *She saved my life.*

"I want you to know that your lady-friend got a little roughed up yesterday. That happened when she beat up the guy who was assaulting you. From what I hear, if I ever go to battle, I want her on my side. Right now, she's being checked out over at the UCSF Medical Center in your city. Although she has four broken ribs, everything else is fine. Well, that is, except for the new beauty mark she acquired on her jaw."

"What?" Luke exclaimed.

"The attacker caught her with his elbow. It caused a gash a couple of inches long. But the plastic surgeon at the hospital did a great job of stitching her up. He assured me that when it heals you won't be able to see where it was. In the meantime, I've sent a dozen roses to her with a note from you saying, 'Get well soon.' I signed it, 'Fondly, Luke.' Then, I added a post-script: 'I can't wait to see you and thank you in person. I'll be stopping by to check on you Sunday.'"

"Why not tomorrow?" Luke's jaw dropped in disappointment. "I'm feeling pretty good now."

"I'm glad you are," Claymore said, "but the hospital administrator says it will take another day to complete your physical. I want you to know I'm taking care of arrangements for you to see her then. . . Oh, and one more thing, when Robin and you have recovered, I want both of you to be my guests at the lavish Coronado Beach Resort. Have a good day, Luke."

Luke was impressed. *My God, I've never been treated so royally.* Then another thought came to mind. *Claymore wrote my note to Robin and signed it "Fondly." I never would have done that. But it's sure sounds better than "Sincerely."*

CHAPTER FORTY-TWO

The Same Day

It was midmorning the next day after Luke had been speaking long distance with Sterling Claymore. Diego and Cam had returned to the demo site to join Rafa in a cellphone call with El Jefe concerning his plan to kidnap Luke.

Aware that their conversations might be tapped by the Feds, they used Rafa's new disposable cell phone. Despite this, an informer on CM3's payroll still managed to keep Dutch Schultz advised of what Rafa and his group were up to.

Cam was impressed with the range of the Los Lomas cartel's tentacles throughout the western hemisphere. Luke was to be released from the Zuckerberg Hospital sometime after noon Sunday and would be taken to the UCSF Medical Center on the Parnassus Heights campus to visit Robin. This was the perfect opportunity to kidnap him.

Becoming aware of this, El Jefe unveiled his plan to nab the neurologist. "Once Luke arrives at Robin's room, a member of my team will distract the duty nurse. This will allow Diego and Cam to enter the room dressed as nurses. They can overwhelm the couple and paralyze Luke with a drug. Then two goons waiting in the corridor with a gurney will cart Luke to the EMT area and load him on a bogus ambulance to rush him away. So, on the day after tomorrow, my team will meet Diego and Cam at the Starbucks across the street from the hospital. They'll bring with them everything needed for the kidnapping. That includes nurse's garb, drug paraphernalia, and so forth. By meeting at eight in the morning, you'll have more than enough time to review every aspect of the plan and have a walk-thru of the hospital premises. I've explained everything to Medellin and told them the demo can't take place until Monday afternoon. They're not happy with it being postponed, but what can they do. I said there were some last-minute problems with the SoulTaker which had to be addressed. They know if something should go wrong with the device, we'll all be up shit creek. While this delay is stressful, it helps us assure the demo will be a huge success."

After the call ended, Rafa said that since the Feds could be intercepting all of their conversations, he ordered Diego and Cam to also switch to new disposable cell phones. Then he grimaced as he said, "Don't let El Jefe's lack of emotion fool you. He may seem calm, but he's fuming inside. Once I saw him act like that just before he cut a guy's throat. If we screw this deal up, my neck is on the line. El Jefe could kill me and maybe you two, as well."

Due to the pressure of what was at stake, the atmosphere had become stifling. Rafa's intense stare at his companions forced them to look away.

Cam gulped as he exchanged a worried look with his partner. His risk-reward philosophy had just turned deadly serious. The ache in his gut seemed as real as if a knife was tearing his bowels to shreds.

Under his breath, Diego muttered a sarcastic smart-ass response to his uncle. "Yeah, yeah, we got the message."

Immediately Rafa jumped to his feet faster than a hungry cat attacking a canary. The beads of perspiration forming on his forehead revealed the pressure he felt. With an unrestrained response he delivered a healthy whack to his nephew's shoulder. The blow caught Diego off-guard sending him reeling backward. The loss of balance caused him to collapse on the floor. His left knee buckled severely. Regretting what he had done, Rafa tried to help his nephew stand. "Sorry, Son, the stress just got to me. We can't afford to screw this up."

Cam grabbed Diego's other arm enabling the two men to pull him to his feet. Then with an arm wrapped around him, Cam struggled to get him out the door. Wincing with pain, Diego needed his partner's support as he limped tenderly to the car. As they reached the vehicle, he said, "Cam, you'll have to drive. I was sure caught by surprise. I've never seen Rafa act that way. I know he's under a lot of pressure. Guess the strain of playing for such big stakes can make one do quirky things."

A few minutes after collapsing in the car, Diego grimaced in pain as he gently massaged his knee. "That fall triggered an old soccer injury. This could be serious. The swelling's one thing but look at the angle of my leg. You'd better get me to a hospital."

CHAPTER FORTY-THREE

The Same Day

The previous couple of hours were far from what Cam had expected. First, he used Google to find a hospital in the area. But with the likelihood of the Feds now having access to their cell phones it became a priority to follow Rafa's order and replace them. As a result, before taking Diego to the hospital, they stopped by a Target store to purchase prepaid cell phones. With this being done, they had a way to keep in touch knowing whatever was said would remain confidential.

When Diego checked into an emergency room, he learned it would take a couple of hours to determine the extent of his injury. Fortunately, the doctor who examined him knew what he was doing. However, the damage to his knee was more serious than suspected. Diego needed to be on crutches for possibly six weeks as a precaution to prevent a recurrence of the buckled knee. It was recommended that once the swelling subsided, he should have physical therapy. In the meantime, he was fitted with a temporary brace, given pain medication, and ordered to stay off his feet as much as possible.

While waiting for his release from the hospital, Diego had used the time to locate another seedy motel for the night in the vicinity of their demo site.

CHAPTER FORTY-FOUR

The Same Day

The NSA agent was thrilled with the latest report his organization put together concerning the search for Luke and the SoulTaker. They had monitored Rafa's conversation with El Jefe detailing the Mexican cartel's plans to kidnap Luke. Based on what was learned, Hank called Dutch Schultz to compare notes. Both concluded it was in their best interest to cooperate by sharing information.

Dutch acknowledged rescuing Luke from Diego's room at a San Francisco motel and had taken him to an area hospital for an extensive medical evaluation. And if he was found to be basically healthy, except for memory problems, he would be taken to visit Robin at her hospital.

Hank realized this situation was the perfect opportunity to capture the two men who had originally confiscated the SoulTaker and Luke. Dutch complimented Hank on pursuing this mission since the Agency had the authority to apprehend the bad guys and CM3 already had the glory of freeing a high-profile target. Besides, the usefulness of the SoulTaker was only good if Luke was there to operate it.

By the conclusion of the conversation, Hank was as upbeat in this investigation as he had been with any other in recent memory.

With the input from Dutch, he felt well prepared to handle the challenge. Plus, he had plenty of manpower and time at his disposal to work out contingencies. He looked forward to settling his score with Cameron Dalton. This time he would not let that guy slip away.

CHAPTER FORTY-FIVE

March 1

Several hours earlier, Cam and four of El Jefe's men met to rehearse the operation to take Luke hostage at the UCSF Medical Center where Robin was staying. Since their run-through, the men had split up to avoid drawing any attention to working together.

Because of the injury Diego sustained from Rafa, the plan to recapture Luke had been revised. This meant Cam would be pulling off the caper with four men he had never met. He felt uncomfortable because, not only did their leader have difficulty in understanding English, but he also didn't know if he could trust them.

Having probably four hours for the event was to start, Cam waited in the nearby Starbucks. He was bored and wanted to have the job over. While he fiddled around with a caffè latte and two glazed donuts, he decided to phone Diego. "How's the knee coming along?"

"The pain's tolerable since I took another oxytocin. You know, Cam, today is one of the most important days of our lives. Sorry you have to do this part without me. But you'll handle it fine."

Cam replied, "Things are all set. We've had our walkthrough and El Jefe's plan is a good one. I just wish I could have put together my own team. Hell, the leader is the only one who can speak English. I guess the other three are reliable and know what they're to do. But my vibes aren't the best right now. I don't trust a guy who can't look you in the eye when we're going over the details."

"Don't let the feeling get to you. Their leader knows how important this is. With this much money on the table, El Jefe's going to send his very best."

"Yeah," Cam replied unenthusiastically. "Anyway, that son-of-a-bitch Luke won't get away. This time I'll be sitting right next to him when we do the demo."

Diego chuckled. "I've got to admit he was pretty clever coming up with a code that changes daily. Thank God Rafa got the meeting moved to Monday. That gives us plenty of time to have everything ready. Too bad it couldn't have been sooner."

Rolling his eyes with delight and smiling, Cam said, "Just think a week from now I'm going to be sitting on a beach in Baja with a margarita in one hand and the other on the knee of a senorita."

After ending the call, Cam replayed his earlier meeting with El Jefe's men. The Mexicans had been waiting for him when he arrived at the delivery entrance to the hospital. Alfonso, their leader, was the only one conversant in English. Cam's first observation was how physically similar he was to this leader. *We're both tall and burly built. But there's something about him that I don't like.* The other three Mexicans were on the skinny side and of average height. Alfonso, being a take-charge man, had explained the abduction plan. Then he and Cam carefully did a walk-thru. Robin was isolated in a ward on the west wing. At that time another gut reaction had hit him. The place seemed too quiet. But he brushed this off as nervousness over this being the most important job of his life. In a storage area down the hall from her room, hospital gowns and masks were stashed in a laundry cart. The only staff member in that vicinity covered the nurse's station. With no traffic in the area, it would be easy for Alfonso, two of the team and Cam to don hospital dress and slip into Robin's room unnoticed. They would inject Luke with a sedative, toss him in a laundry cart and wheel him to the emergency entrance. The fourth member of the team would be waiting to hide him in the bogus ambulance. After going over the plan, Cam had been told to wait at the café across the street until Luke made his appearance.

Now, about four hours later, Cam's phone buzzed. "It's time to get this show on the road," Alphonso said. "Luke should be here in less than an hour. Come on over, we're hiding around the corner from the emergency entrance."

As Cam was about to leave his table at the café, another surge of anxiety struck him. His vibes warned him. *Something isn't right. I think I'm being set up.* Experience had taught him to listen to his gut.

CHAPTER FORTY-SIX
The Same Day

The NSA agent believed today could mark a watershed moment in his law enforcement career. He now had an opportunity to rectify the mistake of letting a sought-after criminal slip through his fingers. This blunder had also cost him the chance to end the nationwide search for a brilliant scientist and his invention.

Breaks in this case finally seemed to be going his way. The wiretapping of Rafa's cell by NSA agents enabled him to develop a scheme to apprehend the bad guys. Robin was going to be the bait to catch Diego and Cam as they attempted to nab Luke. Thanks to this information Hank became aware the culprits knew Robin's location and of Luke's plans to visit her. Learning what he did yesterday had given him plenty of time to arrange a surprise welcome.

By late last night Hank had worked out a plan. The hospital administrator was informed and agreed to cooperate with the strategy. Since Robin's room was in a part of the hospital where the other patients had been removed, the staff was limited to one person. During the time Hank anticipated Diego's attack, between one and three Sunday afternoon, the nurse would be replaced by an NSA agent; one would cover the nurse's station and a half dozen more would hide close to Robin's room as well as the emergency room area where the bogus ambulance was to be parked. The trap was so tight not even a mouse could go undetected. The perps would be drawn into Robin's room and then caught before they could do any harm.

Hank had spent the night in close proximity to Robin's room. This event was too important for him to miss. Early this morning, when he noticed some suspicious characters in the vicinity, he notified his teammates that the place was being checked out by the bad guys. It was their rehearsal for abducting Luke. The NSA team would remain out of sight to avoid contact until the kidnappers made their move. In the meantime, Hank felt it was best to inform Robin about what was expected to happen.

It was shortly after one o'clock when Hank noticed a flurry of activity taking place in Robin's area. From the TV monitor at the nurse's station, Hank saw three masked men enter her room. The larger man wearing a lab coat had to be Cameron Dalton. He was accompanied by two others who were too short to be Diego. Immediately he saw Cam pull a gun and order Luke to move to a chair away from Robin.

Hank was well prepared. He knew what had to be done and fast. He signaled four of his agents to rush Robin's room with guns drawn and was only a step behind them as they entered. Seeing his target, he yelled, "All right, put that gun down!... Now take off your mask."

The leader complied by setting his weapon on a nightstand. When he removed his mask, Hank was flabbergasted. Instead of seeing Cameron Dalton, he saw a husky Mexican—someone he had never seen before. "Who in the hell are you?"

"My name is Alphonso."

"Alphonso what?"

"Sanchez. Alphonso Sanchez. Who are you?"

"Hank Mitchell, National Security Agency," he replied flashing his NSA identity card. "Where's Cameron Dalton? He was supposed to be with you."

"Chickened out at the last minute. Said he'd wait for me to bring Luke Pope to him."

"You mean he's in the area?"

"Yeah, he's probably hiding downstairs in the ambulance outside the emergency ward."

"How about Diego Reyes? Where's he?"

"Don't know anything about him. . . The job was to snatch Pope, keep him alive and turn him over to Dalton."

"You guys are under arrest."

Next Hank phoned his other agents to tell them what had happened. He ordered them to seize the bogus ambulance parked near the EMT drop-off. Hopefully, Cam Dalton would be there, too.

As Hank escorted his prisoners down to the lower level to join his other agents, he felt disheartened. It was like a balloon having suddenly lost all its air. *Holy shit, I thought this case was going to be over today. I wanted to end my career on a high note. There's no way I'm going to retire now; not until I get both Cam and Diego. Even if we nab Cam now, we still need to bring in Diego. Why wasn't he here? Where in the hell is he?*

By the time Hank reached the emergency entrance, the ambulance had been impounded along with the fourth member of El Jefe's team. The only people who remained missing were the important ones: Cam and Diego.

Hank and one of his aides took the El Jefe leader to a private room in the EMT area. During the interrogation Alphonso said, "My boss ordered me and four others to work with two gringos to capture a tall, skinny guy from the room of Robin Hunt. But now that you've caught us, I want to ask for mercy. Our mission failed and no one got hurt so couldn't you just look the other way and let us go."

"Why in the hell should I do that? Why would I ever grant you leniency?"

"Well, what if I helped you get Cam Dalton?"

"And how about Diego Reyes?"

"Reyes never showed up. Somehow, he got injured and couldn't be here."

Hank thought. *What the hell. Getting one of them is better than nothing.* So, he said, "I'll make you a deal. If you can help me, get Cam Dalton, I'll speak to the judge on your behalf."

The Mexican leader replied, "That sounds fair to me. Here's what I know. Dalton is anxious to hear of our success. He's got to be around here someplace. If he wasn't by the ambulance, he's probably at the Starbucks across the street."

Once the NSA team had the other four bad guys in custody, it was decided Hank would take one of his men and the Mexican leader to go after Cam.

Alphonso suggested, "We should slip into the place using the back entrance and surprise him."

CHAPTER FORTY-EIGHT
The Same Day

Cam's nerves showed as he jitterily tapped his fingers on the café table. After another glance at his watch, he gazed across the street in the direction of the hospital. *The kidnapping of Luke should have been finished long ago. Why haven't I heard about it by now? Luke must have arrived at Robin's room. Was the snatch successful? Alphonso should have called to say they had him. I'm sure he was pissed at me for not helping. I just couldn't do it. Something didn't seem right. And I have to trust my gut which is right more often than not.*

Just then, his peripheral vision spied three men advancing towards the back door of Starbucks. Fortunately, he had tucked himself away in a far corner of the shop where he could see both entrances. It was near the hallway to the restrooms where he could hide if necessary. From the corner of his eye, he spotted Alphonso and someone he recognized from a few days earlier. It was the cop who had wrestled him away from Robin; the guy who beat him up when he was capturing Luke. As inconspicuously as possible, Cam slipped away from his table and headed down the hall towards the restrooms. There was no other way to escape. He darted into the men's room and hid in one of the two stalls. He perched on top of a toilet so that his feet could not be seen if someone checked below the door. Suddenly, like a crowd chasing a wounded animal, they charged into the restroom and pounded on the stall doors. Holding his breath, he shut his eyes as if that might help from being discovered. No such luck. The toilet door started to squeak open. "All right Dalton. The jigs up. Toss your weapon on the floor and come out with your hands up." Cam complied. As he meekly stepped out, he said, "Well, Agent Mitchell, fancy meeting you again. Looks like you've got me this time."

The agent's reply was simply a subtle smile.

Less than an hour later, the prisoner was seated across from Hank in the interrogation room at a nearby police station. After a few niceties and a review of Cam's dilemma, Hank said, "You and your associate, Diego Reyes, are in a heap of trouble and are running out of time to get things straightened out. Kidnapping is only one of your troubles. We've got a pretty good handle on what you've been up to. If you don't cooperate, I'll see to it you won't see the light of day for the next hundred years. Now for starters, we need to know where the SoulTaker equipment is and how to find your partner Diego Reyes."

Speaking as bravely as he could, Cam said, "I can help you a lot, but first you have to help me. You have to cut me a deal."

"Any deal depends on how good your information is and how well we can protect the confidentiality of Luke Pope's invention. You're not in much of a position to negotiate."

"You don't have much time either Agent Mitchell. And if you somehow managed to tap my phone in the past hour, you'd realize we no longer need Luke's help. Diego's been busy. He's confident he has come up with the formula to operate the SoulTaker. All he needs now is to give it a try." Cam was not telling the truth, but decided this was the best he could come up with at the moment.

Hank replied, "Dalton, you're blowing smoke. Luke is safe and he's the only one who knows the code. Now the only way you can help yourself is give up the machine and help us get Diego. So, Detective, whose side are you on now?"

Cam gulped. He thought: *if I cooperate, I might possibly get off with only a few years in prison.* Believing this was his best choice, he said, "My part in this caper hasn't really harmed anyone. If you could guarantee dropping all charges against me, I'd give you the SoulTaker and help you track down Diego."

Hank gave a hearty roar and replied, "There's no way we can do that. All I can do is put in a good word for you. Maybe it could minimize your incarceration to a few years. Well, how about it?"

As their eyes met, Cam nodded and Hank offered his hand to seal the agreement.

Cam took it.

Then they worked out a plan for Cam to call Diego and report successfully abducting Luke.

"How did it go, Cam?" Diego asked as he answered the call from his partner. So eager to hear the response, he nervously charged ahead, "Is everything all right? I expected to hear from you some time ago."

"Yeah, yeah, I know," Cam said. Then, uneasily, he added, "We got it done. Mission accomplished. Luke is sleeping like a baby thanks to the tranquilizer I gave him."

In a buoyant mood, Diego charged ahead. "I've got good news, too. I finally came up with the formula Luke uses to operate the machine. By playing around with the numbers, I figured it out. You didn't know I was such a math whiz, did you? The computation is based on the day of the month. Once I enter that code, we're set to go... Come on over to the site. Rafa just brought me here a couple of minutes ago and when you come, we'll have set up the device and have it ready to go. It'll be nice to have Luke around, but I doubt we'll need him." Diego's arrogance came through the connection loud and clear. Then he added, "How soon will that be?"

How absurd! Cam's face was masked with agony. *You're telling me we could have done this fucking thing without Luke. Jesus Christ, Diego, we had it made. Now our dreams have been replaced by free room and board at the big house.*

Looking at his watch and getting approval from Hank, the detective said, "Five-thirty or six at the latest. . . Say, Diego, so you didn't even need to use the operating manual?"

"Huh?" Diego replied automatically, without thinking. Then, it hit him. Suddenly, it dawned on him. "Right, you can forget about the manual." Hearing the key phrase 'operating manual' was the signal to be used if Cam had run into a problem. *Things aren't right. He's warning me to get the hell out of here.* To confirm what he thought he had heard, Diego replied, "Right you are, I didn't need to use the manual."

"Good, glad you figured it out. See you soon," Cam said.

As Diego ended the call, his hand gave a slicing motion across his throat. There was fright in his eyes as he said to Rafa, "The deal's off. Cam's been caught by the Feds. We've got to get out of here before they show up." Rafa had overheard the entire conversation. His eyes locked on his nephew with a stare of devastating defeat. Nothing else needed to be said. Their dreams of unimagined wealth had been dashed. But far worse was that their lives were in danger. The botched attempt to kidnap Luke had cost the cartels hundreds of thousands of dollars. They would be tracked down regardless of how long it took.

In less than an hour, Cam accompanied by Hank and a host of NSA agents pulled up outside Rafa's new demo site. Thankfully, the uncle was used to always having a backup plan in mind. As soon as Diego had heard Cam's warning, he decided to keep the SLT hidden, and they fled. Minutes later they had a perfect view of what was taking place from the top of a neighboring building about thirty yards away. The scene looked like an army of ants scurrying around following the queen ant's orders. The Feds covered any escape from the front and back entrances to the building. Hank and a handful of agents escorted Cam to the front door.

Watching the activity below, the nephew said, "What did I tell you. Cam saved our skins."

"Yeah, that's the end of our sweetheart deal. Not only do we lose a fortune, but our lives might not be worth a plug nickel. We'll be on the run for the rest of our days." Then Rafa explained how the cartels reacted to major setbacks. It meant the two of them needed an escape . . . and fast. The more Rafa thought about it, his chance of surviving was nil. They would track him to the ends of the earth to exact vengeance. Maybe the only thing he could do was use a contingency plan he had long filed away to save his nephew.

CHAPTER FIFTY
The Same Day

Several hours later Hank returned to Robin's hospital room. After capturing Luke's kidnappers, he had left Robin and Luke under the protection of NSA agents. He now told the couple what had happened in the attempt to capture Diego, Cam and the SoulTaker.

In detail, he described the particulars of the plot Diego Reyes and his uncle had undertaken to steal the SoulTaker and sell it to countries who are enemies of the US. He explained the arrest of Cam. The good news was that the sale of Luke's invention to enemy countries had been prevented thanks to the cooperation of NSA, the FBI and CM3. Furthermore, he reported the SoulTaker was missing and its operations remained a secret. Unfortunately, both Diego and his uncle Rafa Perez were still at large. But Hank was optimistic that it would only be a matter of time until they were apprehended. That was, unless the cartels got them first.

Another reason for Hank's visit was to thank Robin for helping crack the case. "I really appreciate your help, young lady. Thanks to you, I can retire on a high note. My final act will be to see that NSA presents you with a letter of commendation making you an honorary member of the agency. And Dr. Pope, or should I say 'Luke', congratulations on winning the heart of such a loyal fan. I hope you let her know how lucky you are to have her as a friend."

Luke beamed as his face turned crimson. As usual, he nothing to say, but his glance at Robin conveyed how much she meant to him.

After Hank left, Luke leaned close to Robin at her bedside. Being a man of few words, he tenderly touched her shoulder as he spoke. "He said it all for me."

She smiled despite the soreness experienced from the beating Cam had given her. Although the pain killers dampened some of her overwhelming joy, she had never felt so fulfilled in her life. "You might not know it, sir, but you're a hard man to track down," she answered in a teasing way.

Luke slid his chair closer to her bed and grasped her hand. "Robin, I don't know how to thank you."

"You already have," she said pointing to the vase on the nearby stand. "Thanks for the beautiful roses you sent. As for the nice note you included, signing it 'fondly' was an unexpected surprise. Something like 'sincerely' is what I might have guessed."

Once again, his face reddened. "Some things happen for a reason. It's finally made me realize how much you mean to me."

"Well, if I'd have known that earlier, I would have tried harder to stop you from seeing that Internet woman. I hope you've learned a lesson."

With a sheepish look, Luke turned away. "I certainly have." Unsure about what to add, he looked into her eyes and said, "By now you know I can't help my being such an introvert. Women make me uncomfortable. I just felt I needed someone to share my life with and didn't know how to go about doing it."

"Well, Buster, you should do your trolling closer to home. Especially, when you work with someone who thinks the world of you. But just to clarify our relationship, I ain't gonna be running out any more to buy Dutch Brothers coffee for you!"

They both laughed and the grip between their hands became firmer.

Staring at the sutures on her jaw, Luke said, "When the scar on your face heals, I'm hoping it'll leave a beauty mark. Then every time I see it, I'll be reminded of how you saved my life."

In a playful manner and using her Clark Gable "Gone with the Wind" impersonation, she said, "'Well frankly Scarlet, I don't give a damn.' Leaving a little blemish behind might be alright. We'll look like twins." Her finger touched the obvious scar on his jaw that he received during his scuffle with Cam.

After a moment, they shared what each had gone through for the last several days. Then once more Luke apologized for his foolhardiness in chasing women when the person he most cared for was with him five days a week. This led them to explore the possibility of building a relationship while working together. Obviously, both were hoping the bond between them could develop into a serious and meaningful connection.

CHAPTER FIFTY-ONE

The Same Day

As Robin was about to be released from the hospital, Luke received a phone call from Sterling Claymore. He wanted to meet the two of them in person. He offered to pick them up in his company plane the next morning and fly them to his office in San Diego.

The CEO said, "Luke, I've been very impressed with your accomplishments. You are a very creative, young man. I appreciate your willingness to take the time to visit me. We've got a lot to talk about."

"Thanks for your invitation," Luke replied. "Robin and I look forward to finally meeting you in person. I can't tell you how much I am indebted to you for having your security man save my life."

After ending the call, Luke turned to Robin. "This will be a treat for both of us. He's one of the most powerful chief executives in the country. Phil claims he has the financial wherewithal to do wonders for our image in industry and educational circles."

*   *   *

The next morning, Monday around ten, Claymore was waiting in his executive office door to greet the couple. "Welcome to the home of the nation's number one pharmaceutical. I trust you had a good flight." With a firm handshake and a generous smile, he added, "It's wonderful to finally meet both of you. Luke, thank God you survived that horrendous ordeal. I was worried something bad might have happened to you." Then giving the inventor's arm a friendly squeeze, he said, "Young man, your achievements are most impressive."

"I . . I . .," Luke began to stutter, but Robin was there to take over.

"Mr. Claymore, I can't thank you enough for rescuing Luke."

"My pleasure," the CEO beamed. "Please come in. We have lots of exciting things to talk about."

The view from the fortieth floor stunned both of the guests. Robin did her best to suppress a gasp as she took in a panoramic view of the Pacific Ocean and San Diego from a height of five hundred feet. Another murmur followed as her attention was drawn to the CEO's well-appointed workplace.

When Claymore directed them to a grouping of posh chairs, Luke's jaw dropped at the sight of a cart displaying Dutch Brothers coffees. Quickly he noticed it included a variety of energy drinks.

The CEO declared, "Luke, I want you to know that Dutch Brothers has given us a franchise and your Aftershock drink has been added to our menu. Their shop will be across the hall from your new laboratory. I'll need some input from both of you in order for us to make final decisions on your décor. Scott will be officed next door. He's been working on the preliminary plans for your lab and is anxious to see if they meet with your approval."

Robin gave Luke a curious glance as if to say, *I didn't know we had a deal to work here. Guess he figures we'd be on his payroll since he plans to manage SoulTaker and anything else you intend to invent.*

Her partner was thinking precisely the same thing. It caused him to say to the CEO, "Sir, we may end up working with your company sometime, but I don't plan to work for you. We're quite happy running the neurology lab at JIT and reporting to Phil."

The CEO replied, "Luke, I haven't had a chance to tell you about the agreement Phil and I worked out in your absence. Since SoulTaker is going to be such a moneymaker, I've agreed to give the university twenty percent of its sales and donate five million a year for as long as we have exclusive rights to selling your product."

"That's news to us," Luke said. "I know this arrangement may be hard for Phil to turn down, but he would never agree to give up the rights to my invention until I figure out a way to protect people's privacy." *Sounds like you've been trying to take advantage of him by promising lots of donations to the university. What you're telling me is not going to fly.*

With a sneer, Claymore felt the inventor needed more convincing. He said, "Let's sit over here and get down to business...Luke, Scott has told me you are truly a genius. I can't tell you how I'm looking forward to the SoulTaker demo. How soon will that be? I can hardly wait to—"

"Mr. . . Mr. Claymore," Luke interrupted, "I need to bring you up to speed on what's happening. I'm sure you know, the SoulTaker is gone. When the Feds broke into the site where the demo was to take place, a thorough search did not find it. It was like it disappeared into thin air. Diego and Rafa have also disappeared. In addition to that, Phil has told me that everything in our lab pertaining to the SoulTaker is gone. He and his staff conducted a thorough search of the lab, my office, and my computer. Even my backup files are gone. The place was ransacked and stripped clean. It's like my invention never existed."

During Luke's account, Claymore had risen from his chic easy-chair, wandered to his floor-to-ceiling windows and stared into space; all the time slowly shaking his head in dismay.

Luke continued, "You might not like to hear this, Mr. Claymore, but if I were to work on the SoulTaker, I'd have to start over at the very beginning. I don't want to do that. This project has taken a lot out of me. I'm thinking, it's probably just as well that I feel this way. All along I've had the feeling my invention gave too much power to whoever controlled it. People have the right to privacy; especially when it comes to having someone get into your mind and use that information in ways you never intend."

"Hold on a minute," the CEO said, "you've developed something for the world that can benefit society in so many ways. You don't have the right to take it away."

"I don't, huh? Just watch me. . . Maybe a time will come when people will be more respectful and considerate of others. But we're not there yet and I'm not going to share this secret until we've figured out how to protect a person's privacy."

"Luke, your attitude is absurd. When word gets out that you are destroying such a great advance in neurology, you'll be ridiculed. Your peers will call you an egotistical flake."

"I know there's goodness that can come from my invention. I just have to figure out how to resolve this dilemma. I'm certain there's a way to make it work. Time will give us the answer. Eventually a solution will come. Until then, I'm going to let it set. Let it incubate."

"That's not a good idea," the CEO replied forcefully. "Abbott is eager to get the thing out. He's looking forward to the financial support I'm going to give the university."

Luke turned to his partner, "Come on Robin, let's get out of here." Then he stared into Claymore's eyes and in a calm and resolute tone and said, "Sir, I don't need you and neither does Phil."

As the couple proceeded to the office door, the CEO's face turned bright red. With a snarl, he said, "The hell you say. You're going to regret this decision. Until you come to your senses, you'll have to muddle along without any support from me. Some day you and Phil will come back to me with your tail between your legs. Then, I'll think long and hard about entertaining any grandiose scheme you come up with. I can't take such disrespect from a whippersnapper like you. This meeting is over. You'd better get to the airport in a hurry before I change my mind about flying you back to wherever you're going."

CHAPTER FIFTY-TWO

March 2

Before leaving on the flight to Palo Alto, Luke called Scott to inform him of the discussion he and Robin had with Claymore. "Sorry we didn't have a chance to see you while we met with your boss. It seems we have a difference of opinion on how we're going to work together."

"Yeah, I know," Scott said. "I just heard from him. He's already put the two of you on his persona non grata list. I'm sure you've learned, it's either his way or the highway. It seems working with him might be out of the question. I hate to see that happen. Luke, would you consider letting me continue to work with you guys?"

"That's exactly what we'd like to hear, Scott. I know Phil feels the same about you as we do. Why don't you slip out of there and join us as soon as you can?"

"Gee, thanks Luke."

After a few minutes of being lost in their own thoughts, Robin said to her partner, "Luke, I'm proud of you standing up for your principles. You handled the situation perfectly. I know you'll figure out what must be done with the SoulTaker. There has to be a way to use it for the good of mankind, but to do so while protecting personal privacy at the same time. It would be tragic if the public did not benefit from your invention."

"I'm optimistic that I can eventually come up the with the solution," Luke said. "As I told Claymore, I just have to let the matter incubate. But in the meantime, I could have another problem. Am I going to be targeted and forced to show someone how to use it?"

For a while, both seemed to be groping for an answer. Then, suddenly with a twinkle in her eyes, Robin blurted out, "I've got it! Luke, you are the only person in the world who knows everything about the system and has the code needed to operate it. Right?"

"Yeah."

"What if there was a way to claim you no longer have any SoulTaker documents and you'd be telling the truth. You could also admit that due to your amnesia, you've forgotten whatever you knew about your invention."

"Then I could say the SoulTaker is strictly a figment of someone's imagination."

"Well?" Robin asked.

"Well, what?'

Luke beamed at the thought: *What a great suggestion. Everyone is aware I'm recovering from amnesia and there is no certainty that my memory will ever fully return. So, if I gave Robin the SLT info I've hidden at home, no one would ever be able to reconstruct the invention. That would even include me.* This led him to say, "By God, Robin, you've got it. All we have to do is for you to stash the SoulTaker stuff away in some secure place for the time being. Then, never let me or anyone else know where you hid it. But my darling, that brings a new twist into play. . . That means if I ever wanted to resurrect the SoulTaker, I'd have to be in your good graces."

"Precisely," she said. "Well, shall we do it?"

"Absolutely."

*　　*　　*

Robin recalled how, a few weeks ago, Luke had hidden the SoulTaker at the Desert Vault in downtown Palo Alto. Well, she decided to do the same thing.

The following day after returning to Palo Alto, Luke turned over to Robin the SoulTaker files he had kept at home. She then took all of it downtown to the Desert Vault. She opened an account under the name: Mrs. Robin Pope. When the clerk at the vault saw the name, she had one comment. "I just moved here a month ago and I'm curious about one thing. Are there a bunch of Popes who live around here? They're fast becoming my favorite customers."

CHAPTER FIFTY-THREE

The Same Day

It was mid-afternoon on Monday when Dutch phoned Claymore with good news. "Well, Chief, mission accomplished."

"You got the device and everything that goes with it?" the CEO asked.

"You bet. As far as I can tell it's all intact."

"Good God, Dutch, that's terrific. I haven't heard a word about what's been going on over there until a few minutes ago. My security department just reported the Feds arrested a group breaking into a warehouse in San Francisco. It seems that included some foreigners having visas that were about to expire. They thought it might be where the SoulTaker demo would be happening. If that was the case, I figured you'd be there."

"You're right. I was in the middle of it," Dutch bragged. "Yesterday, I managed to stay on top of the situation by tapping into Rafa Perez's cell phone. Here's how it happened. Diego texted his uncle to say his combination to activate the SoulTaker wasn't working. So, he and his partner Cam knew they had to kidnap Luke once more to get the right code. Until they got him, they hid the parts of the SoulTaker in a carton stacked in the warehouse. Diego told Rafa very specifically which carton held the device. He gave him the number written on the box. When I learned this, I knew stealing it was going to be a piece of cake. And since I knew the precise time that the demo was to take place, I just blended in with the other authorities in my FBI jacket waiting for the scientists to show up. When they unlocked the door, the Feds attacked at once.

I slid inside with the other Feds who charged the site like a bunch of hungry vultures. When they were shocked at discovering the setup was not complete, I headed for some cartons by the front door. It only took a second to spot the box marked with the number holding the SoulTaker. I grabbed it and was out the door in a flash. No one paid attention to me because everyone was interested in the commotion going on in the warehouse. As soon as I was in my car, I ripped open the carton and found the three SoulTaker boxes."

Dutch continued, "There's been a hell of a lot of competition to learn what's been happening on the SoulTaker case. Everyone was eavesdropping on everyone else. The Frisco police were checking on what the Feds were doing and the cartels were keeping tabs on the government agencies. Right now, I'm speaking to you on a burner phone. The last thing I want is for anyone to know what I've got."

"Congratulations, Dutch, you've done a hell of a job. I knew you could pull this off. Now all you have to do is to get on our plane located at the KSFO, that's the San Francisco International Airport. They've been planning to pick you up for several hours. I told them to just sit tight and you'd be there as soon as you could. Well Dutch, there's one other thing. I've got a present waiting for you when you arrive at Montgomery-Gibbs."

"Present?"

"Yeah, your brand new Ferrari F8 Tributo. It's gassed up and ready to go."

"Holy Shit, I can't believe it."

"You know me, Dutch. I'm a man of my word. . . Let's see, it's almost three now, which means you'll get here before six. I've got a meeting at my office that should end about seven or seven-thirty. How about bringing our new baby to me then? That'll give you time to take a little spin up the PCH to La Jolla. That's where you love to drive, isn't it?"

"Yes sir. I can hardly wait to try it out."

* * *

This was a perfect ending to a perfect day. With the SoulTaker at his side, Dutch drove the winding roads near La Jolla. His favorite route was the seven miles of coastline along the Pacific Ocean. Tonight, he was experiencing the thrill of 710hp in a car he could never have imagined owning. With his Ferrari snaking along the highway, a glance at his watch showed 6:10. *That gives me about an hour before I have to head back to the office.* He tromped on the accelerator encountering another curve. The cornering triggered the hair on his arms to stand at attention as the acceleration pressed him back into his seat. Feeling the g-force was addictive.

The setting sun reflected off the glistening roadway, due to an earlier rain, gave him a surreal feeling of fulfillment. His spirit was uplifted. Suddenly, without knowing it, he was airborne.

* * *

The clock on Claymore's office wall chimed eight times. *Where in the hell are you Dutch? You promised to be here half an hour ago. I'm tired from the excitement of waiting to see the SoulTaker. My pilot told me you landed more than two hours ago. And he said you were so excited to drive your new car that you sprinted to where it was parked.*

Twenty minutes later, the CEO could wait no longer. For some unknown reason, his gut told him to check with the highway patrol. A friend at the CHP answered his private number on the first ring, "Oh, hello Mr. Claymore. This is ironic, I was about to call you."

"Yes?"

"One of your people had an accident near La Jolla. Dutch Schultz is his name."

"Yeah, he's in charge of my Security Department. What's happened to him? I hope he's alright."

"He's been pretty banged up. Got some broken bones and is unconscious. But a medic told my trooper that he'll survive. But I can't say the same for his car."

"Is it totaled?"

"Could be. It got hung up in the pines. Seems like the limbs of those fir trees broke its fall. Then it ended up upside down teetering on a cliff. They're lifting him out of the wreckage right now."

"I'll be over to see him right away."

As soon as the CEO hung up, he called his pilot who flew the company helicopter. "Hey Jeff, I've got an emergency. I'll see you at the bird as soon as you can get there. The highway patrol will give us our destination."

After ending the call, the CEO's thoughts turned to Dutch's prize possession, the SoulTaker. *He's got to have it with him. According to what he had learned from Diego's text to Rafa, the device is operable. All we'll need to know is the code to make it work. Christ, any neurologist worth his salt can figure that out in a New York minute.*

CHAPTER FIFTY-FOUR
Six Months Later

Finally, a well-deserved vacation was in process for the newly-retired NSA agent. Hank Mitchell had always wanted to travel to Mexico in style. And this week-long adventure to Cabo San Lucas was due to the generosity of Sterling Claymore III. The CEO was grateful for the role Hank played in helping Dutch rescue Luke and recovering the SoulTaker.

On his final day of sightseeing, Hank was accompanied by a luscious senorita CM3 had hired to be his guide. They ended the evening at an offbeat bar noted for Baja's best margaritas. She insisted the trip would not be complete without a drink at a scenic view of the sunset where the Sea of Cortez meets the Pacific Ocean. As they shared a cocktail under a star-filled night, Hank had never felt so totally at peace. The hectic chase to rescue Luke and his invention was a distant memory. He briefly reflected on his success and felt no remorse for never bringing Diego and his uncle to justice. Surely, the cartels would have given them their due. His tranquility was briefly interrupted by a glance at the bartender who seemed to look so familiar. Their eyes locked momentarily. Hank instinctively rubbed his eyes as if he was hallucinating. *Good God, that can't be Diego!* When he reopened his eyes, the man was gone. *It's sure funny how your mind can play tricks on you.*

At this same moment, at the same location, Hank's nemesis was experiencing the same feeling. *Jesus Christ, I must be seeing things. That can't be the NSA agent that got Cam.*

Hurriedly, Diego dropped to his knees behind the bar and duck-walked around a lattice wall out of sight. He thanked God that six months of rigorous physical therapy had enabled him to no longer need crutches. After a deep breath he cautiously peeked around the corner once more to confirm what he thought he saw. That man had turned his attention to the lady seated next to him and they returned to their conversation. There's no question. *This definitely is Hank Mitchell. I can't believe it. Our meeting like this must be a coincidence. But I can't take a chance. His stare says that he's recognized me.*

Less than an hour later Diego had gone to his apartment, cleaned it out and was heading to La Paz. For the past three months he had been living in a dream world. For the first time since his escape, he felt free of being discovered by authorities or the cartel. He had a good paying job and a senorita who adored him. Now he would have to start all over. He prayed this was not the way he would have to spend the rest of his life or worse, like his uncle who ended up in a landfill.

As he maneuvered the asphalt in the isolated and tranquil moonlight, his thoughts returned to wondering about what happened to the SoulTaker he had hidden at the demo site. In the many months since it was lost, no mention of it had ever been made again. Returning to look for it was too dangerous. By now it could have travelled to some location where cocaine was king.

Never could he have ever imagined that some frustrated scientist was still trying to unlock the code to activate it.

About the Author

Jerry Maples grew up in Cedar Rapids, Iowa. He received a B.A. from Cornell College and an M.A. from the University of Iowa. After twenty years in banking, he owned and operated an art gallery in Milwaukee.

For fifteen years he has been writing fiction novels. The subjects deal with current social issues — euthanasia, illegal immigration, and a pandemic. His most recent story tells of discovering a piece of the cross upon which Christ was crucified.

Jerry is a widower enjoying retirement while continuing to write in Tempe, Arizona.

www.ingramcontent.com/pod-product-compliance
Lightning Source LLC
Chambersburg PA
CBHW021244260626
47155CB00004BA/1296